DOOMED AS DOOMED CAN BE?

"And how did you find the Hales?" asked Gerard as he and Evangeline made their way down the drive at a brisk trot.

"I found them every bit as nice as I did yesterday," said Evangeline, trying to keep the nervousness out of her voice.

"Miss Hale has a good deal of spirit, and her brother is a likable fellow. Quite brave, also. He once saved one of the Miss Amberquails from a charging bull."

"My," breathed Evangeline, and she imagined Mr. Hale in a suit of armor.

"Yes, he is quite the most dashing fellow in the neighborhood. I suppose now that he and his sister have made your acquaintance, we shall see much of them this summer. I suppose the only way we shall have you to ourselves is if we lock you away and tell visitors you are not at home," he continued, and smiled at her wickedly. She gasped and he chuckled. "Don't be such a widgeon, Cousin. I was only teasing you. Come. If we are to beat the rains, we had best pick up our pace." He spurred his horse to a canter, and Evangeline's mare followed suit.

She looked at the gray clouds devouring what was left of the blue sky and shuddered . . .

D1351904

Miss Plympton's Peril

Sheila Rabe

JOVE BOOKS, NEW YORK

MISS PLYMPTON'S PERIL

A Jove Book / published by arrangement with
the author

PRINTING HISTORY
Jove edition / September 1994

ISBN: 0-515-11453-7

A JOVE BOOK®
Jove Books are published by The Berkley Publishing Group,
200 Madison Avenue, New York, New York 10016.
JOVE and the "J" design are trademarks
belonging to Jove Publications, Inc.

PRINTED IN THE UNITED STATES OF AMERICA

10 9 8 7 6 5 4 3 2 1

For Melinda—
after eight books together,
don't you think it's time?

Chapter
1

"*I am being held a prisoner in this house! Please help me.*"

"Oh, there you are, my dear!"

Miss Evangeline Plympton jumped. "Oh, Papa," she said. "How you startled me!"

Mr. Plympton sat down next to his daughter on the drawing room sofa, and she reluctantly shut her book. "Reading yet another novel?" he asked.

Evangeline nodded. "It is a very good one. I highly recommend it to you. It is about an heiress who is captured by her wicked relatives and held prisoner until she agrees to marry the son of the house. I have just reached the part where she has written a cry for help and plans to slip it to a neighbor at a dinner party."

Mr. Plympton smiled indulgently. "Who is, no doubt, a handsome young man."

Evangeline was amazed. "Why, Papa! How did you know?"

"Never mind, child," said Mr. Plympton. "This heroine is very clever. But no less resourceful than my own daughter would be in such a situation, I am sure."

Evangeline's fair cheeks turned pink with pleasure. "Oh, Papa," she said.

"And I am sure the young lady can be no prettier than my little girl," he added, looking dotingly on his daughter. "With those golden curls and blue eyes you look like a storybook princess. Your mother would have been proud to see how lovely you have become. And, speaking of relatives," Mr. Plympton continued. "We have had a most surprising communication from one of ours."

Evangeline tossed her book on a nearby table. "Uncle Archibald is coming for a visit?" she guessed. "Oh, how delightful!"

Her father shook his head. "No, dear child. This is no relative from my side of the family. I have had a letter in the afternoon post from none other than Lady Bane, your mother's cousin in Devon."

"Why does she write to us?" wondered Evangeline. "I thought Mama's relatives wished to have little to do with us."

Mr. Plympton folded his hands over his paunchy middle. "That has always been true," he agreed.

"Because you had once been a man of business."

He nodded. "In my younger years I was not considered so great a catch—a man from an untitled family with only a moderate income. Your mother definitely married beneath her, and so I always told her."

Evangeline loved to hear how her parents had met at a subscription ball in Bath, how her father had swept her mother completely off her feet. She continued the story for him. "Then you made your fortune."

"A most ungenteel thing to do," he said. "Alas, your mother's family never found me acceptable." He sighed. "Naturally, it was an easy thing to completely lose touch with us after her death. They had rarely seen us when she was alive." He smiled and patted his daughter's hand. "But we were happy enough, weren't we, my little buttercup."

Evangeline assured him she had, indeed, been happy.

And so she had. Her mother hadn't missed the circles in which she once moved, and although her health had been delicate, she had been content with her husband and her child. Mr. Plympton's parents had doted on Evangeline, his older brother had treated her like the child he never had, and the servants had adored her, and done their best to aid her family in spoiling her.

Because Evangeline hadn't lacked for love from her father's family, she rarely gave her mother's relatives a thought. The few times they had visited, she considered them more curiosities than anything else. "Why does Lady Bane write to you now?" she asked her father.

Mr. Plympton beamed in a way which could only be described as triumphant. "They wish to see you, my dear."

"Me?" gasped Evangeline. "Whatever for?"

"Why, to make up for past neglect, naturally," said her papa. "Your cousins are most anxious to reestablish old ties, long broken. I am sure if your mama were alive, she would be pleased to see such a happy circumstance. It saddened her not only that her parents wished to see so little of us, but that her dear cousin, Augusta, also chose to cut us." Mr. Plympton sighed happily. "Ah, but here is a happy ending, indeed. Old sins forgiven. Old wrongs righted. And when they see my little buttercup, they will all regret having had so little time with us these past years."

"Do the Banes wish to come visit us, then?" asked Evangeline.

"No, no. They wish you to come to them at Deerfield Hall."

Here, indeed, was adventure! And heaven only knew she had experienced little of that, thought Evangeline. Her papa worried so about fortune hunters meeting her and taking advantage of her innocence that she sometimes wondered if she would ever have her London season. But now, to go to Devonshire, as the guest of the Baron and

4

Baroness Bane, it was all very exciting! "When do I leave, Papa?" she asked eagerly.

"They wish you to come to them the end of June. Lady Bane expresses the hope that you will remain with them for the summer."

"Oh, my," breathed Evangeline. "May I have some new gowns?"

"Most definitely," said her father. "We can hardly have you going to our grand relations looking like a nobody. And jewels. I should think you will want to take the rubies I bought you and the sapphires as well. Miss Maxim can help you pick out gowns. She seems to be very good at knowing how a young lady of quality should go on." Mr. Plympton's face took on a wistful expression. "If your mama were here she would know what things you ought to take."

Evangeline patted his hand. "Never mind, Papa. Miss Maxim will know."

And Miss Maxim did, indeed, know. She assisted Evangeline in ordering a large assortment of gowns in sprigged muslin and the soft colors befitting a young lady; morning gowns, walking gowns, evening gowns, even a ball gown, the purchase of which caused Evangeline to crow with excitement.

"Now, don't allow your hopes to soar too high," cautioned Miss Maxim. "I am sure your papa will tell Her Ladyship that you are not yet officially out."

"Which I should be," put in Evangeline.

"That is as it may be," said Miss Maxim. "However, the fact is, you have not yet made your debut in society, so Lady Bane might feel hesitant to introduce you to too much social activity. But she may have a small party or two."

"With dancing," added Evangeline excitedly.

Miss Maxim nodded indulgently. "With dancing," she agreed. "So it would be best to be prepared. I am sure your papa would wish it."

"And I shall wear my sapphires," decided Evangeline. "They will look nice with a blue gown."

"Oh, dear," said Miss Maxim. "I must remember to speak with your father about jewels."

"But I already have jewels," protested Evangeline.

"Yes, but the ones you have are hardly proper for a young lady. A nice pearl necklace will be much more the thing."

"But I like my sapphires," protested Evangeline. "And I have never yet had an opportunity to wear them."

"There will be opportunity after you are married," said Miss Maxim firmly. "Meantime, you do not wish to appear to be anything less than a lady of quality."

Evangeline was appalled at the thought. "Gracious, no!" she agreed.

"Then ostentatious jewelry must be avoided at all cost. Young ladies have the glow of youth with which to make themselves lovely, and heavy, ornate jewels can only distract."

Evangeline was very impressed by this speech. "Oh, Miss Maxim, thank heaven I will have you to guide me." Miss Maxim shook her head and Evangeline's brows knit. "But you are coming to Deerfield Hall with me, are you not?" Even as she said the words, she knew the answer.

"Governesses rarely go visiting with their mistresses," said Miss Maxim. "In fact, there is something which I have been meaning to tell you."

"You're not leaving!" guessed Evangeline, horrified.

Miss Maxim nodded. "I am afraid so." Evangeline began to cry, and Miss Maxim laid a comforting hand on her arm. "Now, dear, don't cry. My job here is done. You are a young lady now. Your papa intends to take a house in London for the Little Season. You will be busy with balls and routs and finding a husband, and you certainly shan't need a governess for such activities."

"But what shall I do without you?" wailed Evangeline.

Miss Maxim smiled. "Why, you shall enjoy your visit to your relatives and your come-out." Her smile turned wistful. "And I shall move on to my next charge."

For a moment Miss Evangeline Plympton realized that life was not always fair, and she felt badly that she stood on the threshold of so much adventure and good fortune, while poor Miss Maxim only stood on the threshold of a new job. It surely couldn't be easy being a governess.

But then Evangeline soon forgot the sad fate of Miss Maxim and her fellow governesses and became preoccupied once more with her own upcoming adventure—the trip to Devonshire. What were her cousins like? She remembered so little of them. She had a vague memory of being brought down to the drawing room as a small child and being paraded before a slender woman and a large man. Were they merry people like her father and Uncle Archibald? She hoped so.

Shortly before her departure she learned that her abigail, Wilson, was to accompany her on the trip, and that made her feel better. And Papa was sending them in his fine, well-sprung carriage with the bright yellow wheels and the matching yellow door with the family name emblazoned on it. That should impress the Banes!

"That should impress those cousins!" predicted Cook the morning of Evangeline's departure. "When they see her, the spitting image of her mother, God rest that poor woman's soul, dying so young as she did. Well, we never know when we're going to go, I always say. When she were alive there was none prettier in the whole shire than our missus. And now here's our young miss with all those yellow curls and those big blue eyes. She'll have every boy in Devon head over ears in love with her, mark my words."

"And don't go giving your heart to the first young jackanapes who bids you good day," her father cautioned Evangeline during breakfast. "And don't forget to write the moment you have arrived and let me know how you get on and how you like your fine cousins."

"Of course I shall write," said Evangeline, smiling at her father.

He sighed and said, "I shan't rest a moment till I know you are safely arrived."

"I wish you were coming with me," she said.

"I was not invited, and rightly so," said Mr. Plympton.

"What will you do all by yourself?" worried Evangeline.

"Oh, I shall find plenty with which to occupy myself. Don't fret for your old papa. You just go and show our fine relations what a lovely young lady you've become."

And so she went. In the fine, big carriage with the yellow wheels and the bright yellow door that proclaimed her a Plympton. And her relatives were not impressed when the carriage came to a stop in front of Deerfield Hall.

"Only look what the child arrives in," said Lady Bane with a shudder.

Lord Bane joined her at the window and frowned. "Expensive, though," he said. "It appears she's brought a maid."

"God alone knows what her hair will look like when she removes her bonnet," predicted Her Ladyship. "We can return the maid along with the carriage."

They took their seats in the drawing room and waited for Miss Plympton to be shown in. "Where is Gerard?" queried Her Ladyship petulantly.

"I imagine he will be in shortly," replied Lord Bane, unperturbed. "You can hardly blame him for not rushing to be present."

"I most certainly can blame him," snapped Her Ladyship. "It is his responsibility to be here."

"And here I am," said a voice from the door. A handsome young man strolled into the room. His mother looked him up and down, from his dark, short cropped hair, past his starched and intricately tied cravat and finely tailored coat, to his highly polished Hessians. "It is so good of you to join us," she said sarcastically.

"Under the circumstances I would agree wholeheartedly," he said and came to kiss her cheek.

She had no time for more than a scowl before the butler announced Miss Plympton. Lady Bane set aside her irritation with her son and turned a smiling face to the door. She rose and went to greet Evangeline, holding out both hands to her. "Welcome to Deerfield Hall, my child. What a pleasure it is to see you with us at last."

Evangeline had only time to register an impression of grandeur as she entered the drawing room, with its fine old furniture and thick draperies. She did not notice that the draperies were faded and the carpet on which she trod was thin in places.

She saw, instead, three people, all imposing in

their own way: two dark men, the older one quite large, and this handsome yet fearsome-looking woman, who was speaking as though they had been waiting for years to see her, instead of having only just written.

And what a sinister smile the woman possessed! Why does one side of her mouth seem to droop? wondered Evangeline. It is as if to smile at me is a great effort, she thought, and felt suddenly nervous.

In spite of her misgivings, she dropped a curtsy, and informed Her Ladyship that she was happy to be at Deerfield Hall.

"No more than we are to have you," said Her Ladyship. "And I am sure you will remember my husband, the baron." Evangeline curtsied again and greeted the master of the house, trying not to look afraid, even though she found his saturnine face and awesome bulk intimidating.

"Very pretty," approved the baron in a deep voice, and she sighed inwardly in relief. What she would have done if she had not received his approval she was not sure. Perhaps she would have turned and run.

She forced her nervous eyes to move to the young man. He must be her third cousin, Gerard. Smaller than his father, but with the same dark, brooding looks, he seemed only slightly less intimidating. He certainly was handsome, though!

He took her hand as his mother introduced him, and his touch sent the most delightful tingles racing up Evangeline's arm. She looked up at him, slightly bemused, but managed a smile. The one he returned was small indeed, and Evangeline's own smile shrank. A cold young man, she decided, and felt disappointed.

"I am sure you would like to wash and have a rest after your long journey," said Lady Bane.

"Oh, I am barely tired at all," Evangeline assured her.

Her Ladyship continued as if she had not heard. "We will have a dish of tea at five o'clock. Grimley will show you to your room."

Evangeline bit her lip, feeling foolish and gauche. She suddenly found herself wishing she had not come to this place.

Such a big old mansion, she thought as she followed the butler up the stairs. It was rather depressing, really, almost as much so as her reception had been. She remembered now her first impression of the Hall when she'd seen it out the carriage window; dark and sinister, and stubbornly resistant to all attempts at modernization. One wing had appeared very old, with crumbling stone held up by masses of ivy. She hoped they weren't putting her in that wing of the house.

She was relieved to find herself shown into a very nice bedroom, far from the crumbling part of Deerfield Hall, and the sight of the large room with the thick carpet, the dressing table, escritoire, and canopied bed did much to restore her spirits. This was a charming room.

She went to the window and looked out. The late afternoon sun shone on a large expanse of sloping lawn, and beyond that, a formal garden, complete with a multitude of rosebushes, a maze, and a fish pond. She sniffed, sure she could smell the roses all the way up to her room, and ran to the escritoire to write her father and tell him of her safe arrival.

"I know I will be most happy here," she concluded, "for I have been given a charming room with a view of the lawn and flower garden. Lady Bane was very kind in her greeting and asks to be remembered to you." Well, she thought, I am sure Lady Bane would have asked to be remembered to Papa had she thought of it. And it will please him to read it.

The appearance of a maid with water and a soft clearing of the throat from Wilson forced Evangeline to abandon her letter. "I must close now," she continued, "as hot water has been brought up for me, and Wilson is most anxious that I wash the dust of the road from my face, although I am sure no dust crept inside our carriage. Then I must rest before tea, as Lady Bane has instructed. I don't understand why I must rest when I am not a bit tired, but I know if Miss Maxim were here, she would agree with Lady Bane, so I will rest. Besides, at present there is nothing else to do. I hope this letter finds you in the best of health and relieves any anxiety you may have felt over my safe arrival. I am here safe and sound, and I am sure I shall enjoy myself immensely."

And so she would, she decided half an hour later as she lay down on her bed. She must be more tired than she had realized, and the mind played funny tricks when one was tired. She had, most likely, imagined the lack of warmth in Gerard's smile and the sinisterness of Lady Bane's. These were her relatives, after all.

Unbidden, the thought came to her that the heroine in her novel, *The Captive Bride*, had gone to relatives as well. And what wicked people those relations had turned out to be! Her heart began to dance nervously. "I will not think such thoughts," she said aloud and closed her eyes.

Evangeline didn't remember falling asleep, but she realized she had when she opened her eyes to find Wilson bending over her. "Would you like to get up and change into a fresh gown for tea, Miss Evangeline?" suggested Wilson.

Evangeline rubbed her eyes. "What time is it?" she asked.

"Half past four, miss."

"Oh, my!" cried Evangeline, jumping out of bed. "We had best hurry. I should hate to be late joining my cousins on my first day with them. Whatever would they think!"

"They would think you tired from your journey, miss, and that you chose to sleep rather than take tea."

"You are right, of course," said Evangeline, relief flooding through her. "Whatever would I do without you, Wilson?"

Wilson flushed pink under her mistress's praise. "You would do just fine, I'm sure."

"Well, I don't think so," insisted Evangeline. "I am truly glad Papa sent you along with me. Now, let us hurry. Bring my new sprigged muslin. That will look nice."

Evangeline looked very nice, indeed, when she joined the family for tea, with her hair simply done and a ribbon threaded through it. But Lady Bane was obviously of the opinion that those she considered her social inferiors could do nothing right, including dress themselves. "You look very pretty, my dear," she said, and Evangeline knew immediately Her Ladyship did not approve.

"Thank you," she murmured and perched on the edge of a chair.

"My dear child, please relax," said Lady Bane. "You look poised for flight. We wish you to feel comfortable in our presence."

"Oh." Evangeline blushed and slid a little farther back onto the chair.

"That is much better," Her Ladyship approved. "Do you find your room satisfactory?"

"Oh, yes," said Evangeline. "It is quite pretty. And such a nice view from the window!"

Lady Bane nodded. "There are few formal gardens in Devon to equal ours here at Deerfield Hall. I am sure Gerard will want to show it to you after tea."

Gerard smiled, but it didn't look to Evangeline to be a very enthusiastic one, and she wondered why. Did he find her unattractive? Papa had always told her she was pretty, but then, papas could tend to be prejudiced, she supposed.

Lady Bane was talking. "I have hired a maid who will be able to do wonders with your hair."

Was it her hair, then, that made her appear unattractive to her cousin?

"I think, perhaps, your abigail won't mind returning home tomorrow," Her Ladyship continued.

Evangeline stared at her hostess, struck dumb by such a sudden and high-handed action. Was this how things were done in great houses? Oh, dear. She already felt so at sea, and now they wished to send Wilson home. Who would she have to talk to, to confide in? "But how will she get home?" asked Evangeline, bringing up the first polite objection that came to mind.

Her Ladyship dismissed Wilson's transportation with a wave of the hand. "She can ride the mail coach. Or, perhaps, your father has need of his carriage? If you have a letter to your father, she can carry it for you."

"Excellent idea," approved Lord Bane.

"Of course, any further letters you have you may give to myself or my husband, and we will be happy to ensure they are sent home," added Her Ladyship.

"Thank you," said Evangeline in a small voice and took a sip of tea.

The conversation turned to horses. "Do you ride, Miss Bane?" inquired Gerard.

"Come, Gerard," said his mother. "We must not be so formal. Evangeline is your cousin."

Evangeline smiled encouragingly at the handsome Gerard. "I should be very happy if you called me Evangeline," she said.

"Very well," he said stiffly. "Evangeline. Do you ride?"

"I am not very good," she began.

Lady Bane was shaking her head and smiling in mild contempt. "Neither was your mother," she said. "I used to tell her she should practice her riding skills, for riding is something a lady may safely do for most of her life, and it is so very good for the figure. Ah, well, I suppose she had little enough need after she married your father. I am sure she was too busy running the house."

"Mama had a great deal of time to ride after Papa made his fortune," said Evangeline, quick to spring to her mother's defense.

Distaste was plain on Lady Bane's face.

"I am sure Evangeline is a good rider," said Lord Bane. "We shall have to see about finding you a suitable mount," he told her.

"More tea?" asked Her Ladyship, closing the subject.

After tea Evangeline was only too happy to escape to the garden, even if it was in the presence of the unenthusiastic Gerard. "These roses are all so very pretty," she announced and bent to sniff a white one.

"As is the young lady who stands among them," he said.

Evangeline straightened and regarded him. "That was a very nice compliment," she said. "Did you mean it?"

He looked surprised. "Why should I not?"

She shrugged. "Oh, I don't know," she said.

"Has no one told you before that you are pretty?"

"Only Papa, and my uncle Archibald. Oh, and the servants," she added.

"I find that hard to believe," said Gerard.

"Perhaps if I saw more people my own age, someone might compliment me. If I really am pretty, that is."

Gerard chuckled. "Oh, you are. Believe me. And please accept my apologies."

"Whatever for? Was it wrong of you to compliment me?"

"No. But what I thought when I offered the compliment was obviously wrong."

"And what, pray, was that?"

"Why, that you were fishing for a compliment, of course."

"How could commenting on the loveliness of the roses be considered fishing for a compliment?" wondered Evangeline.

"That," said Gerard, "is something you will come to understand when you have been more about in polite society. I imagine it won't take you long to become an accomplished flirt."

Evangeline knew not what to say to this, so instead changed the subject. "Your parents were very kind to invite me to visit," she said.

A cynical smile appeared on Gerard's face. "Yes, weren't they?" he agreed. "I hope my mother does not offend you with her high-handed ways. I believe she is what is known as a managing female."

Evangeline shrugged. "I remember mama once saying that her cousin was very bossy."

"That is a blunt way of putting it," agreed Gerard, and they walked on. "I am sure you will like the maid my mother has in mind for you."

Evangeline was determined to keep her own maid with her, but she politely said, "It was very nice of your mama to offer to find me a new maid. I suppose Wilson does not quite have the knack of doing my hair as well as some might, but I must say I have always liked it."

Gerard merely nodded.

"I suppose your mama wishes to have my hair looking more stylish before presenting me to anyone in the neighborhood," guessed Evangeline.

"That is most likely so," he agreed. "Although I am sure even my capable mother will find it hard to improve on perfection. Shall we go in?"

Evangeline would like to have lingered at the pond and counted the goldfish, and the maze looked like great fun. But it was clear her cousin had enjoyed enough of her company, so she allowed him to escort her back into the house.

How very odd, she thought as she made her way back to her room. Gerard was nice enough, and certainly had paid her some handsome compliments, but for some odd reason, he held himself aloof. Or was that just his normal manner? She shook her head. A very cold man. A very cold man, indeed.

As she put her hand out to open her door, she had the odd feeling that someone was watching her. She turned to see a child crouched at the end of a row of chairs sitting along the wall, peeking up at her. The child, a little girl with a crop of black curls, stuck out her tongue and ran off, leaving Evangeline to stare after her in shock. Well! she thought. Who could that have been?

Dinner was early and quiet. Lord Bane talked little, and when he did it was mostly to his son, and of fishing. It seemed the two men spent a good deal of time fishing the stream that ran through Deerfield Park. What did the ladies do in their absence? she wondered. The prospect of spending long days tête-à-tête with Lady Bane was not an appealing one, and Evangeline suddenly found herself longing for her own friendly household. Perhaps she could end her visit to her cousins early.

After dinner the ladies left the gentlemen and

repaired to the drawing room. Evangeline seated herself and arranged her skirts. She looked up to find Mrs. Bane regarding her. And with her slightly drooping mouth and those intent eyes, it made an unnerving sight. Evangeline swallowed hard and gave her a tentative smile.

Her Ladyship smiled back, that awful, sinister half smile.

Evangeline swallowed again.

"We are all very happy to have you with us, dear child," said Her Ladyship. "Please forgive me for staring, but I see so much of your mother in you." Suddenly Lady Bane's countenance seemed less stern, less frightening. She looked a little sad.

"I am told I look like her," offered Evangeline.

"She was a sweet creature." Lady Bane shook her head. "More hair than wit, I am afraid, but sweet just the same. And, yes, you do look like her. I would hope, however, you are a more sensible young lady than was your mama." Lady Bane's lips compressed in disapproval. "She never knew where her duty lay, fairly broke her mother's heart when she married your father."

"Mama and Papa were very happy," ventured Evangeline.

"I am sure they were," said Lady Bane tolerantly. "Still, your mama should have thought of her family. A girl should always think of her family and do what is right. That is how I was raised," Her Ladyship finished with a nod.

"As we are speaking of family, I wonder if I

might ask who the child I saw earlier today is," said Evangeline.

"You must be speaking of Minerva, our daughter," said Lady Bane. Her brows lowered in displeasure. "But when did you meet her?"

"I just happened to see her in the hall as I was going into my room," said Evangeline, conveniently neglecting to tattle on the naughty Minerva.

Lady Bane nodded, still not pleased. "Well. If her governess can restrain her long enough, she will be presented to you tomorrow. I have given her permission to come take tea with us."

"I shall look forward to meeting her," said Evangeline.

"I am afraid sometimes she can be rather naughty. I hope she was not misbehaving when you saw her earlier," said Her Ladyship.

"Oh, no," lied Evangeline. "She merely smiled and ran off."

At that moment the gentlemen joined the ladies, and the subject of Minerva was dropped. "Do you sing, Evangeline?" asked Lord Bane.

"A little," replied Evangeline nervously.

"Then let us hear you," he commanded.

"Your mama had such a sweet voice," added Lady Bane in tones that seemed to Evangeline to dare her to sing as sweetly.

Evangeline obediently went to the pianoforte and found some music. Her voice sounded weak and shaky, even in her own ears, and her nervous-

ness caused her to lose her place. She bit her lip
and murmured an apology.

"No need to apologize," said Lord Bane in his
big voice. "You are doing fine."

"Very lovely," added Lady Bane. "Wouldn't you
agree, Gerard?"

"Of course I would, Mother," said Gerard.

There! Evangeline chided herself. See how silly
you are acting. They are all trying very much to
make you feel at home. Stop being such a goose.
And on that stern note, she took a deep breath
and began again, and was able, this time, to finish
her song.

Lord Bane gave his approval, and his lady
informed Evangeline that her voice was every bit
as sweet and true as her mama's had been.
Gerard rose and joined her at the instrument,
offering to sing a duet with her.

And so the rest of the evening passed pleasantly enough, with more music, and finally the
supper tray at ten-thirty. Evangeline went up to
bed that night feeling that her relatives weren't
such a bad sort after all, and that her visit would,
most likely, be pleasant enough, even if Lady
Bane did look like a villainess from a novel.

But that was before she went to climb into her
bed.

Chapter
2

Evangeline let out a shriek.

Wilson, who had just been dismissed for the night, came running. She followed Evangeline's gaze to the foot of the bed, where the covers had been torn off, and let out a startled gasp. There lay a dead field mouse. Wilson looked at her mistress in horror. "Who would do such a thing?"

"I think I know," said Evangeline slowly as a childish face framed by black curls came to mind.

Wilson shuddered. "I will have fresh sheets brought up right away, miss, and change the bed myself. Such a household!" Wilson took a sheet of writing paper from the escritoire and gingerly slid it under the tiny rodent. "But first I will show this to the butler."

"No, wait," ordered Evangeline. It had been a

harmless enough prank, and she had no desire to get the perpetrator in trouble with her formidable mama. "Just fetch some fresh bedsheets. And leave the mouse here."

"Oh, but, miss . . ." protested Wilson, her face wrinkling up in disgust.

"No, it will be fine. Really."

Wilson watched the thoughtful grin growing on her mistress's face. "Oh, now, Miss Evangeline. I know that look," she said nervously.

"After you have changed the bed, please find some paper and ribbon and a small box, will you?"

Wilson looked as if she wanted to protest such strange doings, but she murmured, "Very well, miss," and hurried off.

Within the hour fresh sheets had been put on the bed and a small box wrapped with pink ribbon sat on Evangeline's dressing table. Evangeline took one last grinning look at it and climbed into bed, being careful to put herself as far from the side where the dead mouse had lain as possible. She sighed happily as she burrowed under the covers. Oh, but she was going to have fun staying with her relatives!

The next morning Wilson was doing Evangeline's hair when there was a knock at her door and Minerva made her entrance. She was scrawny and thin-lipped. Not a pretty child, thought Evangeline. "Hello, Minerva," she said. "Do come in."

"I am already in," Minerva informed her.

"So I see. Then please be seated."

Minerva perched on the bed and looked around her as if searching for something. "How did you know who I was?" she demanded.

"Your mama told me," said Evangeline. "Are you looking for something?"

Minerva smiled slyly. "Did you sleep well?" she asked.

Evangeline's smile was equally sly. "I slept wonderfully. Such a comfortable bed!"

Minerva looked none too pleased with this answer and for a moment said nothing. But she didn't remain silent for long. "Are you the goose that lays the golden eggs?" she asked.

What an odd thing to say! Surely this was the strangest child she'd ever met, Evangeline concluded. Of course, she hadn't met a great many children, but nevertheless, she was sure there were few like this one.

"Well, are you?" demanded Minerva.

"I don't think so," Evangeline said.

"You are our cousin, aren't you?" persisted the child.

Evangeline nodded.

"I thought so," said Minerva.

Evangeline decided this was a far from satisfactory conversation and changed the subject. "I have a present for you," she said, taking the small beribboned box from her dressing table. She held it out to Minerva.

The child's eyes lit up, and she jumped off the

27

bed and snatched it from Evangeline's hand. Evangeline watched, smiling, as Minerva tore the ribbon off and lifted the lid.

On seeing the contents of the box the child's eyes widened. She looked at the grinning Evangeline and burst into tears and fled the room.

Evangeline laughed, and Wilson joined her. "Did you see her face?" said Evangeline at last.

"Yes, miss. I should say you taught her a lesson." Wilson turned thoughtful. "But I hope you have not made an enemy of the child. She does not seem to be a very nice little girl."

"She's horrid," said Evangeline. "I am sure I was never like that." She turned to Wilson. "Why do you think she would behave so to me when she does not yet know me?"

Wilson shrugged and resumed pinning up her mistress's hair. "If she is the youngest, that might explain it. The youngest is often a mischief. My little sister was ever a bother. And she was always worst when no one was paying her any mind. Perhaps this child is neglected and bored."

"If that is the case, I can see why she is neglected," said Evangeline with feeling. "If she were mine, I should put her in the attic."

Wilson smiled at this. "I don't believe you would, miss. You are much too kind-hearted."

"That child would turn anyone's heart to stone," replied Evangeline. Having spent enough thought on Minerva, Evangeline checked her reflection in the looking glass. "This will do very well, Wilson," she said. "Now I think I shall venture out in search of breakfast."

Evangeline managed to find her way to the breakfast room, and, on seeing the vast array of silver chafing dishes set out on the sideboard and smelling the good smells, all thoughts of the nasty Minerva flew from her mind.

Lady Bane was already seated and eating a bowl of porridge. "Ah, Evangeline. I trust you slept well."

Once my small, furry bedfellow was gone I did, thought Evangeline. "Yes, thank you," she said. For a moment she considered betraying Minerva then and there, but immediately thought the better of it. It would hardly do to start off on such a wrong foot with her relations the second day of her visit.

"I thought, perhaps, you might like to see something of the Hall today," said Lady Bane.

"Yes, that would be very nice."

"I shall have Gerard show you."

"What am I to show our cousin?" asked Gerard, sauntering into the room.

"Gerard. You are up early."

"I had thought to ride over to Idyllwilde and inform the Hales that Evangeline has arrived."

"I am sure they will be paying a visit soon and can then discover that fact for themselves," said Lady Bane.

"Perhaps Evangeline would fancy a ride this morning," suggested Gerard, undeterred.

Evangeline said she thought a ride would be very nice, but Lady Bane had already ordered the day and saw no need to change things.

"I think it would be a good idea if Evangeline were to learn her way around our home before she is required to learn her way about the country-side," said Her Ladyship.

Gerard gave in, inclining his head to his mother. "As you wish, Mother." He smiled politely at Evangeline. "I am sure you will enjoy seeing our decaying family castle, especially the east wing."

"Gerard!" said his mother sharply. She turned to Evangeline and smiled that unnerving smile. "My son likes to jest. In truth, some of the east wing is in need of repair; hardly suitable for guests. It is little more than unused rooms, at any rate."

"Oh, it is a little more than that," put in Gerard. "The schoolroom and nurseries are there," he informed Evangeline. "My sister's governess has a room there, also."

Lady Bane dismissed the nurseries as being of no interest to Evangeline.

"They might be," argued Gerard. "Doesn't every woman wish to see the nurseries when looking over a house? After all, one never knows whom one might marry; therefore every man's nursery must be of interest." He turned to Evangeline. "Wouldn't you agree, Cousin?"

Lady Bane was looking displeased, and Evangeline didn't quite know what to say. "I must admit," she began hesitantly, "I never before considered such things."

"Then you must be a most unusual young woman," said Gerard pleasantly.

"Pray, pay no attention to Gerard," said Her Ladyship. "He delights in being difficult and upsetting his mama."

Gerard raised an eyebrow. "Was I being difficult? I do beg your pardon." He turned again to Evangeline. "I am sure you would prefer to see the gallery and admire the portraits of our ancestors. We also have a well-stocked library. Do you read?"

"Oh, yes!" said Evangeline excitedly.

"Homer? Ovid?"

"Well, no."

"Are you fond of history?"

"Er," said Evangeline.

"Really, Gerard," said his mama. "Evangeline is hardly a bluestocking."

"Shakespeare, then?" guessed Gerard.

Evangeline nodded slowly. She supposed Shakespeare would do in a pinch.

"Well," said Gerard, "I shall take you there, and you can see what catches your fancy."

Lord Bane didn't appear at breakfast, and Evangeline learned this was because he had breakfasted long before anyone else and was already off attending to estate business.

It would appear Gerard's business for the day was to entertain her, which he proceeded to do as soon as they had finished eating. He showed her the grand saloon, which was a good-sized room, and, he said, often used as a ballroom.

"Do you think your mother and father might have a ball this summer?" asked Evangeline.

"Would you enjoy that?" he asked.

"Oh, yes," she replied.

"Then I am sure my mother will arrange to have one," said Gerard. "Would you care to see the gallery now?"

The gallery was a long, carpeted room, lit by tall windows at either end and containing more portraits than Evangeline had ever seen in one place. "Gracious," she breathed.

"Quite," agreed Gerard.

"Are they all your family?"

"Most of them. Some, however, are friends. Or important connections." Gerard took a few steps and pointed to a portrait of a gentleman in Elizabethan costume. "Robert Cecil was an important family connection, as you can see by the prominent display of his portrait. Our family has always been wise in the connections it made and careful in its loyalties." Gerard's face turned thoughtful. "It is possibly the reason we have been able to keep our lands down through the generations. And this fine hall," he added sarcastically.

"Part of it is in disrepair?" prompted Evangeline, remembering the conversation at breakfast.

He acknowledged this with a nod and closed the

subject by leading her to another portrait. "I am sure you recognize this gentleman."

Evangeline studied the middle-aged man in the fine coat, the satin breeches, and powdered wig of the older generation. "He looks familiar."

"So he should," said Gerard. "It is your grand-father."

She blushed, feeling rather foolish. "So it is," she said. "We saw so little of him." Her voice trailed off, and she searched for something to aid her in leaving behind a subject which could prove embarrassing. She moved to another portrait. "Who is this funny-looking woman? Such a face!"

Gerard was next to her, smiling his cold smile. "It is my great-grandmother," he said.

Evangeline wished the floor would open and swallow her. "Oh, dear. I do beg your pardon."

"For speaking the truth? You are right. She was, indeed, an unattractive woman. But my great-grandfather badly needed funds, and she was well dowered. She brought a much-needed fortune to the family coffers."

It seemed a sad tale. The poor ugly woman must have known she was only wanted for what she could bring to the Bane family.

As if reading her mind, Gerard spoke. "I believe they were very happy together."

Evangeline had seen enough of portraits. She went to a window at the end of the room and looked out. On the lawn below she saw a young woman walking hand in hand with Minerva. The sun glinted on the woman's chestnut curls, making them shine like polished copper. As if feeling someone's gaze upon her, the woman turned to look up at the house, and Evangeline caught a glimpse of her face. "What a pretty woman!" she declared.

Gerard came to stand behind her. "It is my sister's governess," he said.

Evangeline thought of her own dear Miss Maxim and wondered how she was faring in her new position.

Gerard had already turned from the window. "If you have seen enough of the gallery, perhaps you would care to stroll about the grounds a little."

Evangeline was definitely tired of looking at stuffy old pictures of people she did not know. "I shall just get my shawl," she said.

"I think, perhaps, you might not need your shawl," said Gerard. "It looks to be fairly warm already."

"Then I had best fetch my parasol," said Evangeline.

"We shan't be outdoors long. And besides, I think an occasional small amount of exposure to the sun's warmth most salubrious. Don't you?" Gerard was smiling and offering her his arm.

She took it and allowed herself to be led from the gallery.

They went out onto the front lawn. At the far end they saw the governess and her charge sitting on a blanket, sketchpads open, intent on drawing the front view of the Hall.

"Come, Cousin," said Gerard, "and allow me to present you to Miss Farnham, my sister's governess. I believe her to be near your age, and I think she would enjoy talking with you." As if worried his cousin would feel herself above being kind to a mere governess, he rushed on, "She comes from a very old and respected family, but is, alas, fallen on hard times and forced to make her way in the world."

Evangeline was immediately intrigued. "Did her family lose their fortune?" she asked.

"They had little fortune to lose," replied Gerard. "I am afraid Miss Farnham's greatest misfortune is in the sudden death of both her mother and father in a freakish accident only two years past."

"How terrible!" exclaimed Evangeline. "But had she no relatives who could give her a home?"

"She was, I believe, an only child. And rather than impose on her relations, she has chosen to earn her own way in the world."

The poor woman, thought Evangeline. All alone. At the mercy of fate. And now here she was at Deerfield Hall, forced to reside in the crumbling ruins of the east wing. Was it haunted?

"Let us go see how the drawing lesson progresses," Gerard suggested.

Evangeline reined in her runaway imagination and went with him across the lawn.

At the sight of their approach, the young

woman scrambled to her feet, a blush on her face. The poor creature. How nervous Gerard made her! Evangeline could well understand that. There was something about her cousin . . .

Gerard was making introductions, and again Evangeline had to recall her wandering thoughts.

"I am pleased to meet you, Miss Plympton," said Miss Farnham. "I hope you will enjoy your stay at Deerfield Hall."

"Oh, I am sure I will," said Evangeline.

"I hope she goes home soon," said Minerva.

Evangeline's eyes widened in surprise and embarrassment, and Gerard scowled at his little sister.

Miss Farnham's face flushed a deep pink. She turned to her charge. "That was most impolite, Minerva. Miss Plympton is a guest in your house and I certainly cannot have you spoiling her visit before it is even begun. Please tell Miss Plympton you are sorry."

Minerva looked mutinous, but obeyed. Evangeline accepted the reluctant apology, inclining her head, and thought there could be no child on the face of the earth more odious than this one.

Miss Farnham smiled on Minerva approvingly. "Thank you," she said.

"I only do it for you, Miss Farnham," Minerva muttered.

"It is a start," said the governess.

Having done her duty, Minerva made her curtsy, then turned her back on the adults, picked up her sketchbook, and moved away to another spot on the lawn, where she sat down and resumed her drawing.

"You look tired, Miss Farnham," said Gerard. "The child taxes your strength."

Miss Farnham blushed under so much kind attention. She shook her head. "Not at all. It is life that has taxed my strength. Minerva, and the kindness of this family, renews it."

A pretty speech, thought Evangeline. And such kind concern from her cousin. Perhaps he was not such a cold man after all.

Minerva was calling to her governess to come see what she had drawn. "I suppose we had best leave you to your drawing lesson," Gerard said and shepherded Evangeline away.

"Minerva is a beast," he said, as if reading her mind. "But Miss Farnham has done wonders with her."

Evangeline said nothing to this, merely nodded, and Gerard suggested he show her the library. "Where I shall leave you to peruse the books in peace," he added, and she wondered if he was leaving her because he was tired of her company or because he thought her tired of his.

In truth, she had grown tired of her cousin. He certainly was not the merry soul her papa was, and a small amount of his company went a long way.

She spent a good portion of the day in the library, looking for something by Mrs. Radcliffe.

Alas, she could find neither Mrs. Radcliffe nor any other of her favorite authors, and she discovered no subject or title in that vast room full of books that appealed to her.

She had given up the search and was about to leave when Grimley came to inform her that visitors longing to make her acquaintance awaited her in the drawing room. Following him down the hallway, she wondered who the mysterious visitors were. She hoped they were more entertaining than her cousins.

Grimley opened the door and announced her, and she entered the room to find a hearty-looking young man with reddish hair and a strong-looking, ruddy face and a slim young woman with light brown curls and fine gray eyes seated with Lady Bane.

"Evangeline," said Her Ladyship, "this is Mr. Hale and his sister, Miss Hale. They reside at Idyllwilde and are our nearest neighbors."

Her cousin's introduction seemed less than enthusiastic to Evangeline, and she wondered why. The brother and sister seemed an amiable enough pair.

"Evangeline!" exclaimed Miss Hale in sudden raptures. "Just like the heroine in the book."

Evangeline knew a kindred soul when she saw one. She took a seat next to Miss Hale. "You have read it?" she asked eagerly.

"Oh, yes!" exclaimed Miss Hale. "I thought it the most wonderful book ever written."

"Even more wonderful than *Mysteries of Udolfo?*" pressed Evangeline.

"It would be very hard to choose between the two," admitted Miss Hale. She smiled at Evangeline. "I do hope your visit will be a long one, for I can see we will have much in common, Miss Plympton. Do you enjoy dancing? And riding. Are you fond of riding?"

Mr. Hale smiled indulgently on his sister. "How can Miss Plympton answer one question when you immediately throw another at her?" He turned his friendly gaze on Evangeline. What fine blue eyes he had, she thought. And such a warm smile. Not at all like Gerard's.

"My sister was quite excited when she heard we would be having another female residing in the neighborhood, even if only for a short time, for we seem to have few young ladies of quality whose company she can enjoy," Mr. Hale explained.

"Oh, it is not that there are none," put in Miss Hale. "The Misses Amberquail live only five miles south. And they are very nice. But they are both plain, and not at all interested in fashion. And then there is Miss Quinn. She is very beautiful. She had her first London season this spring and is now engaged to a marquess, so naturally she considers herself above the rest of us," added Miss Hale in disgust. "I am to have a season next year," she informed Evangeline. "But I am sure even if I snare a duke, I shan't be so high in the instep as Miss Quinn has become."

"Miss Quinn is a very conceited young lady," said Lady Bane in disapproving tones. She smiled politely at Miss Hale. "Will you and your brother stay and take a dish of tea with us?"

"We would be delighted. Wouldn't we, Edwin?"

Mr. Hale agreed and the bellpull was rung and tea ordered.

Lord Bane and Gerard joined them, and Evangeline noticed how much more lively the conversation seemed with the Hales present. Obviously the Banes stood on good terms with their neighbors, and she was glad to see that, for she hoped to see much of Miss Hale. And, she thought, as she peeped at him from under her lashes, she wouldn't be averse to seeing more of her handsome, smiling brother, either.

Partway through tea Miss Farnham brought Minerva in to officially meet Evangeline. "Minerva, I wish to present you to our cousin, Miss Plympton," said Lady Bane.

"We have already met," said Evangeline, giving the child a level look.

Lord Bane looked surprised, and his lady's eyebrows lowered. Her face suddenly cleared. "Oh, yes," she said. "You saw Minerva in the hallway."

Evangeline gave Minerva a challenging look. "I have spoken with her, too. Only this morning, as a matter of fact."

Minerva's chin jutted out in a show of bravado,

and Evangeline saw she was blinking furiously, determined not to cry.

Shame on you! Evangeline scolded herself. What would Miss Maxim think of such cruel behavior? She smiled at Minerva. "On the lawn today. I admired her sketch of Deerfield Hall."

Minerva seemed to relax and Evangeline smiled. Perhaps the child would take the proferred olive branch and they could end hostilities.

Lord Bane was smiling indulgently on his daughter. "Making our cousin feel at home already, eh? Good girl."

"I cannot tell you how very attentive she has been," murmured Evangeline. At that moment she looked in Mr. Hale's direction. His quizzical smile told her he understood the sarcasm behind the comment, and she couldn't help smiling in return. Mr. Hale's smile broadened, flustering Evangeline and causing her to lower her gaze and take a restorative sip of tea.

The Hales drank their tea and took their leave, but not before wringing a promise from Gerard to bring Miss Plympton to Idyllwilde to pay a morning call the following day.

When Evangeline finally went to her room to dress for dinner, she took with her the sure feeling that she was indeed going to have a most enjoyable stay at Deerfield Hall.

She dressed in record time and made her way down to the drawing room. The door had come the slightest bit ajar, and as she made to enter the room, Lady Bane's voice drifted out to her. "It will never do to have the girl become thick with them. I can tell she is already smitten with the brother. I depend upon you to bring her back in record time tomorrow, Gerard."

Evangeline's brows knit. Why would it not do to become good friends with the Hales? Surely they must be socially acceptable, else her cousins wouldn't receive them. Didn't her cousins wish her to make friends with anyone in the neighborhood?

She stood hesitating at the door, wondering how long she should wait before entering the room. She would hate her cousins to think she'd been eavesdropping on them. She turned at the sound of footsteps behind her to see Lord Bane, bearing down on her, a frown on his face, and gave a start.

"Why are you lingering in the hall, child?" he said, taking her by the elbow. "No need to stand on ceremony. If you wait for Grimley to announce you every time you enter a room, you'll spend a great deal of time standing about with sore feet." And so saying, he propelled her into the drawing room.

Evangeline was sure Lady Bane looked at her narrowly as she entered the room. Did Her Ladyship know she had been overheard?

Before Evangeline could say anything to assure her hostess she hadn't heard a word of her conversation, the butler appeared to announce that dinner was ready.

The evening meal seemed a torturous affair to Evangeline. Lord Bane looked even more dark and saturnine than he had seemed when first she met him, and the friendly look he gave her, she was positive, was a sham. In her nervousness she managed to tip her glass of wine and drench the tablecloth, and although everyone was kind and reassuring, Evangeline could not feel comfortable.

Before the meal was over, the Hales' visit had been discussed at length. "I knew we would barely have Evangeline beneath our roof before they would be over," said Lady Bane in disgust.

Her husband nodded his agreement. "Miss Hale is a silly girl with little to occupy her mind, and her brother makes himself amiable to the point of being a nuisance. But they are well enough liked in the neighborhood."

"Oh, yes," agreed Her Ladyship. "And if one enjoys such flighty types, I suppose they are good enough."

"Our summers have certainly been more lively since they purchased Idyllwilde," observed Gerard. "And our Yuletide as well."

"Yes. Young people do like a little entertainment," agreed his mother. She turned to Evangeline. "We are very quiet here at Deerfield Hall. I hope you may not find it boring."

"Oh, no," Evangeline assured her truthfully.

She had, thus far, not always found her visit pleasant, but she had yet to find it boring. And after meeting the Hales, she was sure she could look forward to many delightful outings. The conversation Evangeline had heard earlier came back to haunt her. If I am allowed out, she thought.

The ladies left the gentlemen to their port and withdrew to the drawing room, where Lady Bane again brought up their amiable neighbors. "I imagine Miss Hale will make a nice friend for you while you are here," she said. "Of course, we will be busy with our own affairs, and there might not be much time to see her," she finished, and Evangeline defiantly vowed then and there to see a good deal of Miss Hale.

The gentlemen joined them, and the rest of the evening was passed playing whist, a game at which Evangeline hardly excelled. But her hosts were patient with her, Gerard explaining the fine points of the game as they went along.

By the time she retired to her bedroom, she was once more chiding herself for letting her imagination run rampant. Her relatives were rather a stiff lot. And naturally they would look down their noses at the neighbors, for, although the Hales were gentry, they were not nobility. But to have seen something sinister in her cousins' behavior had been a little silly.

Evangeline slept peacefully that night and awoke early the next morning with a smile on her face. Still smiling, she rang for Wilson.

Ten minutes later another girl appeared in Wilson's place. Evangeline looked at the rosy-cheeked young woman before her. "Where is my abigail?" she demanded.

The girl looked at her in surprise. "Why, Her Ladyship sent her off over an hour ago. I'm Smith, miss, and Her Ladyship hired me to be your maid while you are here." Her speech finished, the girl turned timid and lowered her gaze to the carpet.

Evangeline sat on the bed and stared at her. "She sent Wilson away, without me being able to say so much as a word to her, or even send along my letter to my father?"

The girl ventured a look at Evangeline. "I believe your maid took that, miss. She found a moment to speak to me before she was sent off, and told me to tell you not to worry, that she would make sure your papa got your letter, and that she would be fine, and that Lady Bane had paid her very well for bringing you here."

Such high-handed ways! After all, Evangeline had never actually agreed to sending Wilson home. "Even if she was only a maid, she was my maid, and I would have liked to bid her farewell," Evangeline grumbled.

The girl bit her lip, then spoke. "It is known in these parts that I have a way with hair. I was abigail to Miss Quinn. Of course, now that she is betrothed to a marquess, she needs a finer lady's maid. But I really am very good," the girl rushed on, "and I know all the latest styles."

So, thought Evangeline, her cousins were going to do all in their power to make sure she did not disgrace them. She supposed if she had turned up with gowns that were unsuitable, Lady Bane would have had dresses made for her before allowing her to go anywhere.

Evangeline sighed. Such condescending behavior! Her relatives must certainly look down on her family. Why ever had they wished her to visit?

Well, she could hardly take out her frustration on this poor girl, who seemed so intent on pleasing. She smiled at Smith. "I am sure we will deal very well together," she said.

Even as she said it, she remembered *The Captive Bride*. Safe in her happy, slightly dull home, that novel had sent cold shivers of delicious fear scampering up and down her spine. Now, once again, the cold shivers began their shuddery race, and it was anything but delightful. In her mind's eye Evangeline saw the heroine, an heiress, just like herself, sent to visit relatives who held her captive until she promised to wed the son of the house. Evangeline remembered how, at the end of the first chapter, poor Kathryn's trusted maid had been sent away, leaving her alone and friendless in the great, crumbling mansion.

Evangeline's heart began to palpitate and she bit her lip. Deerfield Hall was a very big house, indeed. And she suddenly felt very alone.

Chapter
3

Evangeline allowed Smith to assist her into one of her new gowns, then sat unseeing while the girl quickly spun her curls into a new hairstyle.

"There!" said Smith in satisfied tones.

The sound of her maid's voice roused Evangeline, and she forced herself to focus on her looking-glass reflection. She saw the artfully arranged golden curls and smiled with pleasure. "Oh, I like this ever so much better than my old style!" she exclaimed.

"See how it shows off your pretty blue eyes," said Smith, giving a lock of hair one final twist.

Evangeline had to admit that her new maid had much more of a knack with hair than Wilson ever had. But still, she missed Wilson. And reminding herself of that, she made her way down to breakfast.

As before, Lady Bane was already seated at the table, this morning consuming deviled kidneys and eggs. "Ah, good morning, dear child," she said. "I hope you slept well."

Evangeline merely said, "Yes, thank you," and turned to the sideboard.

"You look a little tired this morning," observed Her Ladyship. "We are all unfashionably early risers here, but if leaving your bed so early does not agree with you, you may have a tray brought up."

"That is very kind of you," said Evangeline, thinking that her own company would be preferable to breakfast with the formidable Lady Bane every morning. She helped herself to eggs from a silver chafing dish and joined her hostess at the table.

"I see your hair is styled differently," observed Her Ladyship. "And quite becomingly, too, if I might say. I knew Smith would be the perfect abigail for you. I hope you were pleasantly surprised."

"She is very good," agreed Evangeline, fresh anger at Lady Bane's high-handed ways seething in her stomach. "I do miss Wilson, though," she boldly added.

"Of course you do," agreed Her Ladyship. "I am sure she was a most loyal creature. But really, an abigail must be more than loyal. After all, a lady is no better than her maid."

"Wilson was a very good maid," insisted Evangeline.

"But what were her qualifications? What references did she give? Had she ever been lady's maid to a true lady of quality?"

Evangeline blushed under this barrage of questions and said nothing. Her papa had thought Wilson's references very fine, indeed. But what did her poor papa know of choosing abigails? she wondered miserably.

Lady Bane nodded triumphantly. "I thought so," she said. "Please allow me to assist you in some of these finer things, my dear. I know with your mother gone these past years it cannot have been easy. We should have brought you to us long ago."

Evangeline bridled at this. Was Lady Bane insinuating her papa was not a suitable father? Granted, he had not been nobility, but he had not come from the lower classes, either. So how dare Lady Bane talk in such a manner! "My father was a perfectly good father and I was very happy with him," she said hotly. "And my maid was a perfectly good maid, and it was very cruel of you to send her away and leave me alone and unprotected." Lady Bane looked at her in horror. Evangeline's face turned crimson and she lowered her head. "I do beg your pardon," she whispered. The eggs on her plate swam before her eyes, and she found she no longer had an appetite.

"You are overtired, I am sure," said Her Ladyship stiffly. "Perhaps if you were to rest upon your bed awhile this morning, you would feel better."

Evangeline nodded, unable to speak.

"I shall send a note over to Idyllwilde, telling them you are unwell."

Evangeline found her voice. "No. Please. I shall be fine. I am sure it is as you said, I am just tired. But the fresh air would do me good."

"As you wish," said Her Ladyship, continuing to speak in the prim tones of one who has forgiven an insult but still feels the wrong of it.

"If you will excuse me," said Evangeline, "I think I shall go rest."

Her Ladyship inclined her head, and Evangeline fled the room. But instead of going to her bedroom, she went outdoors to walk about the grounds and mull things over.

The more she thought, the more distraught she felt. Whatever had she been thinking of to speak so to Lady Bane? It would never do to have her relatives know she suspected them of nefarious doings.

And suspect them, she now did. She was no foolish ninny, like Kathryn, the captive bride, had been. That silly heroine had turned a blind eye to all suspicious doings in her relatives' home until it was too late. But not Evangeline Plympton! She was watchful. And clever. They might send away her faithful maid, but they would never achieve their wicked ends.

And what were those wicked ends? A vision of her cousin Gerard's coldly smiling face came to her. Of course! She was an heiress. The east wing was crumbling. They would hold her captive until she promised to marry Gerard.

A terrifying new thought took hold of Evangeline, and she bit her lip to keep from bursting into tears. After that distressing interview with Lady Bane she was most likely perilously close to being locked away this very day.

She must leave Deerfield Hall before it was too late. She would return to the breakfast room and tell Lady Bane she wished to go home immediately.

Evangeline crept back into the house and down the hallway to the breakfast room. She met no servants en route, and was just as happy not to, for the servants, most likely, had all been instructed to spy upon her. She pushed the door open, but her entrance was unheard, for Lord Bane was now in the room with his wife and was speaking in his great bullish voice.

"What do you mean she thinks we have spitefully sent off her maid?"

His wife's voice was low, and from where she stood Evangeline couldn't hear her well. Lord Bane started to pace, and fearful of being seen, Evangeline backed out of the door.

His Lordship's exasperated words came to her

plainly. "I told you, Augusta, that this silly scheme of yours would not work."

So, it was true! They planned to hold her prisoner.

Terrified, Evangeline ran off down the hall as fast as she could go, missing the advice Lord Bane gave his wife. "If you ask me," he said, "we should send the chit packing and be shot of her."

"Don't be ridiculous," said Lady Bane. "It is not every day Providence throws an heiress in one's lap. She has to marry someone. Why not Gerard?"

"She bids to be more trouble than she is worth," predicted His Lordship.

"There will be no trouble I cannot take care of," said his lady. She looked sternly at her husband. "The east wing cannot wait for the exchange to improve."

Lord Bane glowered at her and informed her he had estate business to attend to.

"As do I," she retorted.

Lord Bane harrumphed and begged his wife to tell him no more of *her* estate business, then left her to send for her son.

Abovestairs, Evangeline had reached her room and was now pacing, trying to determine how best to remove herself from her dangerous position. So. It was just as she had first suspected. Her relatives were not the simple, kind people they pretended to be. She was in grave danger. What should she do?

She thought of running away, but tossed aside

that plan immediately. She had no money with her, and it would be most improper to travel alone. And besides, she had paid little attention to her surroundings and had no idea of the name of the nearest town, or in what direction it lay. She was helpless, alone, and in great danger. The Hales were her only hope.

She rang for Smith, suddenly very anxious to ride to Idyllwilde, even if it was in the company of the evil Gerard.

Smith was delighted for any chance to handle her new mistress's fine clothes and made much fuss over Evangeline's fine gray riding costume, admiring the way the short-waisted jacket with its capuchin collar showed off Evangeline's diminutive figure. She even knew how to smartly tie the cravat, which was worn above the lawn shirt with the frilled front, and Evangeline was not displeased with what she saw when she looked at her reflection.

She thought the worried expression in her eyes lent her rather a tragic look. She hoped her new friend would ask if anything were amiss, for that would give her the opportunity to beg Miss Hale's assistance.

Naturally, Miss Hale would offer her brother's aid as well. And Mr. Hale looked so big and strong and capable. A vision came to mind of Mr. Hale pulling her free from Gerard's evil grasp and carrying her off to safety. Yes, she would definitely beg Miss Hale's assistance!

Smith had just handed Evangeline her gloves when a footman arrived with a message from Gerard, telling Miss Plympton he would be delighted to escort her to Idyllwilde whenever she wished. "Please tell him I shall be down in a few minutes," Evangeline instructed, trying to sound calm, and Smith relayed the message.

"I hope you enjoy your ride, miss," said Smith as Evangeline departed.

"Thank you, Smith," said Evangeline. She would not in the least enjoy her ride, knowing what she now knew about this wicked family.

Gerard was already waiting at the foot of the great staircase for her, and smiled his perfunctory smile as she came down. "You look very fetching this morning, Cousin," he said.

Had his mother spoken to him of her outburst at breakfast? She hoped not. "Thank you," she said, trying to make her voice sound cheery. Don't let them know what you suspect, she counseled herself. It is your only hope!

The butler opened the front door, and as they went outside, she couldn't help feeling a little freer than she had only a moment before. "I must say, I am very glad for a chance to learn my way about the countryside," she said. For one never knew when one would have to ride away in the dead of night, and one could hardly do that when one didn't even know her way about in the light of day.

"It is a very pleasant ride to Idyllwilde," said Gerard mildly. "I am sure you will enjoy it."

They walked to the stables, where they found their horses already saddled and waiting. "Father thought this might be a suitable mount for you," said Gerard, leading her to a fat little chestnut mare. Evangeline looked at her horse, and for a moment her heart sank. She wondered how she could ever outrace Gerard's fine black horse on such a poor steed as this should he try to make violent love to her en route to Idyllwilde. Well, she would just have to hope he behaved himself.

Gerard did behave himself all the way to the Hales', and Evangeline felt oddly let down that the wildest thing he did the entire way was to suggest a gallop across a field. Well, he was most likely biding his time, she concluded as they trotted up the tree-lined drive to the house.

Miss Hale had been watching for them and came out of the drawing room to greet them just as Gerard was giving his hat and gloves to the butler. "I feel I have been waiting an age for you to get here," she bubbled. "And I hope you don't intend to go rushing off, Mr. Bane, for I know Miss Plympton and I will have much to say to each other, and I am looking forward to a nice long visit." As she spoke she linked her arm comfortably through Evangeline's and drew her into the room, leaving Gerard to stroll after them. "You will allow me to call you Evangeline, won't you?" she begged. "It is such a romantic name!"

"Oh, yes. Please do," said Evangeline eagerly.

"And you will call me Charlotte?" Miss Hale was smiling, practically dancing to the tea tray, and her lively spirits caused Evangeline's to lift as well.

Mr. Hale joined them in time to hear his sister's words. "Perhaps Miss Plympton doesn't wish to be on such intimate terms with someone she has only just met," he suggested, smiling at Evangeline as if to show her he was only saying what he knew to be polite.

He took her hand, and she smiled worshipfully up at him, knowing she would be safe from her wicked cousin as long as this kind, brave man was present. "Oh, no," she said. "I should like ever so much to be called by my Christian name."

"There, Edwin," said Charlotte. "Now that you have done your brotherly duty, you may be at ease and enjoy our new friend's company." She smiled at Gerard and handed him a teacup. "And that of our old one as well."

Gerard inclined his head and returned the smile, and Evangeline noticed it was less reserved than the ones he had given her. Perhaps, she thought, he has a tendre for Charlotte. Is he being forced to court me against his will?

She didn't have long to think of Gerard, for as soon as Mr. Hale engaged him in conversation, Charlotte addressed her again, and her voice seemed suddenly very serious. "I do believe we have a great deal in common, other than our love of books. I understand your mama has been dead these many years. I have no mama, either."

Evangeline's heart constricted. "Oh, I am so sorry."

Charlotte nodded. "Mama has been gone four years. It is why I have not yet had my season, even though I have really been out these past two years. Poor Papa. It has taken him a long time to recover. Actually, I was to go to my aunt this last spring. She was going to bring me out. But the estate did not do well, and Papa felt it would be prudent to wait one more year." Charlotte lowered her voice. "I think he has been secretly hoping that one of our neighbors might offer for me. But I have managed to discourage them all, for I wish to go to London and make a grand match such as Miss Quinn has made."

"I am sure you will," said Evangeline. Who would not love her new friend? With her lively spirits and lovely looks she was bound to captivate any man.

Charlotte was whispering now. "I think there were some in the neighborhood who wished Miss Quinn would give her hand to their sons. And her rich estate as well," she finished and giggled. Evangeline looked thoughtfully at Gerard, and Charlotte followed her gaze and nodded. "Oh, yes," she whispered. "Gossip has it Her Ladyship was crosser than a bear when Miss Quinn and her fortune escaped." The sudden look on Charlotte's face registered the realization of a social blunder. "Oh, I do beg your pardon," she said earnestly.

"Please do not," said Evangeline, equally earnest, "for I must ask you. That is . . ." She looked nervously to see if Gerard was listening. He and Mr. Hale were deep in conversation. "I beg you to tell me what you think of Lady Bane," she said in a low voice. Charlotte looked at her, puzzled, and she blushed. "It is just that she has such a sinister smile," she whispered.

Charlotte nodded knowingly. "Yes," she agreed. "It quite unnerves me at times. But I believe it was not always so. Edwin says it is some sort of affliction—a palsy which she suffered after the death of her oldest son."

Evangeline's eyes widened. "Gerard had a brother?"

Charlotte nodded and stole a look in the two men's direction. "Oh, yes," she whispered. "And he was even more handsome than your cousin. Everyone expected him to marry well. But he was quite wild. He died one night on his way home from the King's Arms, quite foxed. He fell from his horse and drowned in the stream in only three feet of water."

"Gracious," breathed Evangeline.

"Of course, all responsibility for restoring the family fortune now falls to your poor cousin," continued Charlotte. "I think it must be very difficult to have to marry for money, don't you?

There are so few pretty heiresses. And the ones who are pretty are all quite spoilt."

Evangeline felt a betraying flush on her cheeks. Obviously, Charlotte didn't know she was an heiress. For a moment she found herself reluctant to betray such an ugly secret and tarnish herself in her new friend's eyes.

Yet she needed to confide in someone. And besides, heiresses might sometimes be spoilt, but Charlotte was well read enough to know that they were also often in danger. Charlotte would understand. And if she, Evangeline, didn't speak now when she had the chance, she might not get another. For all she knew the family could be planning to lock her away as soon as she returned to the Hall. "I am afraid I must confess something to you," she began.

But Charlotte wasn't listening. Her eyes lit up and she rose from her seat. Evangeline turned to see a bony, middle-aged man with faded blue eyes and the wig favored by the older generation shaking hands with Gerard. "Papa!" exclaimed Charlotte. "You must meet our new friend, Miss Plympton."

Evangeline fought back frustration as Charlotte eagerly led her father to her. "This is Miss Plympton, the Banes' cousin, come to stay with them for the summer. Is she not pretty?"

Mr. Hale bowed over Evangeline's hand. "Other than my own daughter, I have never seen lovelier," he said, smiling, and Evangeline decided she liked him very well. Surely such a kind man would stand her friend and be brave enough to face the wicked Banes. Now, if only she could find an opportunity to seek his assistance.

Mr. Hale settled into a wing chair, and the conversation turned to summer amusements.

"I think we should have a ball in Miss Plympton's honor," suggested Charlotte.

"A very good idea," agreed her brother, smiling at Evangeline. "And I shall support you in your request as long as Miss Plympton promises to give me a dance."

"Of course," murmured Evangeline, demurely lowering her gaze. How handsome Mr. Hale was! Such broad shoulders! A vision of herself dancing with him played before her mind's eye and made her smile.

"I am sure my mother is already planning such an event," said Gerard, and the happy scene vanished with a poof as Evangeline was brought back to reality. What a wicked thing to say! She was sure his mother was planning no such thing.

"A dinner, then," said Charlotte. "We must have a dinner in her honor. We can invite the Amberquails. And Miss Quinn, if she will condescend to dine with us. And we should take Evangeline on a picnic!" She turned to Evangeline. "Should you like that?"

"Oh, yes," said Evangeline quickly. The more time she spent in the company of others the safer she would be from her cousins.

Edwin Hale turned to Gerard. "It would appear you are doomed to share your fair cousin. There will be no keeping her to yourself."

Ha! thought Evangeline. Just try and lock me away now.

"I assure you, I had no intention of doing any such thing," Gerard replied. He looked at Evangeline. "I was just noticing the sky, Cousin. I believe we are soon in for a shower. Perhaps we should start home?"

Evangeline looked out the drawing room window. It did, indeed, look as if a sudden summer storm were about to descend on them.

As she watched black clouds encroach on the blue skies, she felt a feeling of gloom move over her spirits. She hated to leave this happy, bright house and go back to Deerfield Hall. How she longed for the handsome Edwin Hale to insist they remain, but he merely smiled regretfully.

"Yes, you are right," she said in a small voice. She rose from her seat with great effort. Here she was about to be snatched away before she had an opportunity to ask for help. She took Charlotte's hand and held it tightly. "Perhaps your family could spare you to me tomorrow for a visit," she said, and looked at Charlotte with as pleading an expression as she dared show before her cousin.

"By all means," said Mr. Hale. "If it is still raining tomorrow, you may take the carriage."

Charlotte looked happily at Evangeline, who returned her gaze with one of extreme gratitude.

"If you would care to come for luncheon, I know my mother would be delighted to have you," said Gerard graciously.

Charlotte accepted and Gerard and Evangeline took their leave of the Hales.

"It is very odd," said Charlotte in worried tones after the guests had been shown out and her father had left her alone with her brother.

"What is odd?" asked Edwin, picking over the remains of the tea tray.

"The way Evangeline looked at me when she was taking her leave," said Charlotte. "It was as if she were trying to tell me something."

"It seemed to me Miss Plympton had a great deal to tell you. And you her," he teased.

"Edwin. I pray you will be serious," Charlotte scolded. "When she asked me to come see her tomorrow, she had a pleading look on her face, and she held my hand very tightly, as if she were afraid." Charlotte turned a worried face to her brother. "What can it mean?"

Edwin frowned and looked thoughtful. "I hope she is not in some kind of distress." At last he shrugged and smiled reassuringly at his sister. "I am sure it is nothing."

"Yes, perhaps you are right," said Charlotte doubtfully.

"Would you feel better if I were to accompany you tomorrow?" suggested Edwin.

His sister gave him a sly smile. "Evangeline is a very lovely young lady," she observed.

Her brother's ruddy complexion turned redder yet. With pretended nonchalance he nodded his head in agreement. "And if she is in some sort of trouble . . ."

"She needs a handsome man to come to her rescue," finished his sister. Now Edwin was blushing furiously. Charlotte smiled and laid a hand on his arm. "There now, dearest. I shan't tease you any more. In all seriousness, I am concerned, and it would ease my mind greatly if you would accompany me to the Hall tomorrow. Perhaps Evangeline might feel free to confide in us. And if she is in trouble, I can think of no man more capable of helping her than you."

"And how did you find the Hales?" asked Gerard as he and Evangeline made their way down the drive at a brisk trot.

"I found them every bit as nice as I did yesterday," said Evangeline, trying to keep the nervousness out of her voice.

"Miss Hale has a good deal of spirit, and her brother is a likable fellow. Quite brave, also."

Evangeline's interest was piqued. "Is he?" she asked, temporarily forgetting her fear of her cousin.

"Oh, yes," said Gerard. "He once saved one of the Miss Amberquails from a charging bull."

"My," breathed Evangeline, and she imagined Mr. Hale in a suit of armor.

"Yes, he is quite the most dashing fellow in the neighborhood. I suppose now he and his sister have made your acquaintance, we shall see much of them this summer. I suppose the only way we shall have you to ourselves is if we lock you away and tell visitors you are not at home," Gerard continued, and smiled at her wickedly. She gasped and he chuckled. "Don't be such a widgeon, Cousin. I was only teasing you. Come. If we are to beat the rains, we had best pick up our pace." He spurred his horse to a canter, and Evangeline's mare followed suit.

She looked at the gray clouds devouring what was left of the blue sky and shuddered.

Chapter 4

Lady Bane frowned at the note the footman had presented to her on a silver salver. "I impose on your generosity, dear Lady Bane, only because I know you won't mind in the least," she read, and punctuated the sentence with an indignant, "Humph."

Evangeline was delighted to hear that Charlotte's brother was accompanying her, but wisely kept her feelings to herself.

"Miss Hale is a very forward young lady," said Her Ladyship. "But that is to be expected. Such behavior is what comes of not having a mother to guide one."

Evangeline knew Her Ladyship's words were directed as much at her as her friend, and hung her head.

"Ah, well," continued Lady Bane philosophically. "One must be gracious."

And Her Ladyship was, indeed, gracious when the Hales made their appearance. She assured Charlotte that her brother was a most welcome addition to their table and condescendingly smiled at Edwin as he bowed over her hand.

Evangeline's smile was timid as the young man took her hand, holding it as if it were a rare treasure. And although he held it a trifle longer than was proper, making Evangeline feel very self-conscious, she found herself greatly disappointed when he released it. Such a fine, strong hand Mr. Edwin Hale had.

"You are looking lovely today, Miss Plympton," he said.

"Oh, Edwin," said Charlotte. "It is very silly of you to call Evangeline 'Miss Plympton' when your very own sister is her closest friend and addresses her by her Christian name."

Edwin's face turned pink and he muttered something about being proper.

"Very right," approved Lady Bane, fixing Charlotte with an imposing gaze. "It would be most improper, and I congratulate you, Mr. Hale, on your good sense."

Now it was Charlotte's turn to blush.

Grimley appeared to announce that luncheon was served, and Lady Bane allowed Edwin to lead her in to the drawing room, followed by the chastised Charlotte and Lord Bane, with Gerard and Evangeline bringing up the rear.

After everyone was seated, Her Ladyship seemed to think Charlotte had been punished enough for her forward behavior and inquired politely after the senior Mr. Hale.

Charlotte, obviously willing to forgive and forget, cheerfully replied, "Papa is well. Of course, when we left he was buried deep in a book."

Evangeline saw her chance. She turned to Charlotte, who was seated on her right. "Speaking of books," she said, "I would like very much to loan you *The Captive Bride*. It is a book with special meaning for me." On these last words she looked earnestly at Charlotte.

"Oh, yes," enthused Charlotte. "I have heard it is a most exciting tale—all about wicked people who hold a poor girl captive."

"Utter nonsense," scoffed Lord Bane.

"Oh, but it wasn't," protested Evangeline.

Gerard raised an eyebrow. "Such things happen often in real life?"

"They could," countered Evangeline. "After all, one never knows about people, does one?" she finished, leveling an accusing gaze at her cousin.

"And why was this poor creature being held captive?" persisted Gerard.

"Because she was an heiress," replied Evangeline. "The family wished her to marry their son so her fortune would be theirs."

"I enjoy a well-written novel as much as the

next person," said Lady Bane, "but such vulgar works do nothing for a young lady's mind. Even Miss Austen's work, over which I know many have raved, I found most preposterous. Her heroine was a very rude young lady, and Miss Austen expected a great deal of her readers when she asked us to believe that Miss Elizabeth Bennett and Mr. Darcy should wed at the end of the book after so intensely disliking each other throughout the entire thing."

Evangeline's indignation increased as Lady Bane's speech continued. Not only was Lady Bane trying to throw the Hales off the scent by convincing them of the impossibility of kidnapping an heiress, she was also insulting Miss Austen! It took every ounce of courage Evangeline could muster to speak up against her forceful hostess. She cleared her throat and said, "I enjoyed *Pride and Prejudice*. And furthermore, I think if a lady was rich enough, perhaps it would be tempting to certain unscrupulous people to force her to marry into their family." She felt Lady Bane's wicked gaze on her, and her face reddened self-consciously.

Charlotte looked puzzled. "Was there a kidnapping in *Pride and Prejudice?* I must confess, I don't remember it."

"I believe my cousin was speaking of the other book," said Gerard, "the one with the heiress."

At the mention of her favorite book, Evangeline tried to catch Charlotte's eye so she could throw her a pleading look. Charlotte, however, was smiling at Gerard, and Evangeline bit her lip in frustration and frowned at her plate.

She looked up in time to see Mr. Hale studying her, brows knit in puzzlement. Evangeline took hope. Mr. Hale had seen her distress. If only she could tell him of her plight, he would find a way to rescue her. She tried to tell him with her eyes, putting all the pathos she could muster into the quick, desperate look she shot him.

"All a waste of time, if you ask me," observed Lord Bane. "Sitting about reading novels concocted by men who couldn't seat a horse if their life depended on it, and silly women with nothing better to do. Give me a good fox hunt! That is what I say."

His lady nodded her agreement and changed the subject accordingly.

The current of conversation swirled around Evangeline, whisking away all talk of captured heiresses. Instead, unfamiliar names and places now swam past her. She toyed with her food and bided her time.

After luncheon the elements conspired with her cousins and the cloudy skies spat fat raindrops, making a walk about the garden and a confidential tête-à-tête impossible. In the drawing room the visitors chatted, happily ignorant of the wicked plot hatching within the crumbling walls of Deerfield Hall, and the poor captive racked her brain for a way to tell them.

Before she knew it, her rescuers were announcing their need to return home. "How fortunate we brought the carriage," said Miss Hale, "for this rain shows no sign of letting up." She took Evangeline's hand. "You will come and see me soon, won't you?" she begged. "I feel there are still volumes left unsaid between us."

"Oh, there are," said Evangeline earnestly.

"We must have a picnic!" declared Charlotte. "As soon as the fair weather returns."

Evangeline wanted to scream, "That may be too late!" But she restrained herself, knowing she dared not let on to her wicked relations that she knew about their nefarious plans.

The Hales took their leave and scurried from the front porch into their carriage. After waving a fond farewell, Charlotte leaned back against the squabs and sighed. "That was delightful."

"You seemed to enjoy yourself very much," observed her brother.

"Did I?" she replied, cocking her head.

Edwin smiled. "I should say you did. It would be very considerate of you to save Father the expense of a London season."

"Why, what ever can you mean?" wondered his sister.

"I think you know," said Edwin. "Bane is a handsome devil."

Charlotte smiled. "Isn't he?" She adjusted her pelisse. "But I have no serious designs on him."

Edwin folded his arms across his chest. "As I

suspected," he said. "You are a shameless flirt, dear sister."

"Nonsense!" retorted Charlotte. "But one must ready oneself for London."

"And while one was busy readying oneself, one's brother was observing one's friend."

Charlotte's faced turned serious. "What are you saying?"

"I am saying that I believe you were right. Something, indeed, troubles Miss Plympton."

"My poor dear Evangeline! I wonder what it can be."

Edwin shook his head. "I don't know. Perhaps a clue lies in the book to which she kept referring."

"Oh, my! She did offer to loan it to me, didn't she?"

"I should be happy to ride over and fetch it for you," offered Edwin.

His sister smiled slyly at him. "How very sweet of you," she murmured.

Having done their part in the conspiracy, the clouds left the following day, leaving blue skies and a bright sun. The grounds of Deerfield Hall beckoned, and after a morning spent in Lady Bane's company, Evangeline decided to escape for an early afternoon stroll about the gardens. She knelt by the fish pond and ran an idle hand through the water.

"Be careful," said a deep voice. "A hungry fish might bite your finger."

Evangeline jumped and let out a yelp.

"I am sorry, Cousin. I did not mean to startle you," said Gerard.

Evangeline pressed a hand to her thumping heart and tried to paste a look of composure on her face.

"Would you care for some company?" her cousin asked.

Not yours, thought Evangeline, but she politely said, "If you wish."

He helped her up and they began to walk. "You haven't yet had an opportunity to explore the maze," said Gerard. "Would you care to try it?"

"Yes, thank you," said Evangeline politely.

On their way to the maze, they encountered Miss Farnham and Minerva. Gerard called a greeting and beckoned them with a wave.

Evangeline noticed that the smile Miss Farnham gave them was a sad one. Poor thing. Her delicate shoulders seemed too frail for the burden they carried.

"Good morning, Miss Farnham," said Gerard pleasantly. "How is my sister behaving today?"

Miss Farnham's sad expression had produced a scowl on her charge's face, but Miss Farnham either had not seen it or chose to ignore it. "Minerva has been a very diligent pupil this morning, which is why we are taking a walk."

"Minerva, would you care to show our guest the secret of the maze?" suggested Gerard.

"No," replied Minerva honestly. Her brother

frowned at her. "But I shall," she added. "Come along," she said to Evangeline.

Evangeline did not appreciate being told to come along as if she were the child and Minerva the adult, but rather than make a scene, she obliged. Miss Farnham and Gerard fell in step behind her.

Shortly after they entered the maze, Evangeline realized that Minerva had managed to separate them from Gerard and Miss Farnham. She could hear their voices somewhere behind the hedge. "We have lost your brother," she observed.

Minerva smiled wickedly. "If a person becomes lost in this maze, they could wander for days," she said.

"Stuff," scoffed Evangeline.

"They could be lost and starve to death," continued Minerva.

"Have you been lost?" asked Evangeline. The vision of Minerva wandering forlornly about the maze was a pleasant one, and Evangeline smiled at the thought.

"I could find my way out with a scarf tied round my eyes," Minerva boasted. "But you won't ever get out," she added and dashed off.

"Beastly child," muttered Evangeline as the sound of Minerva's scampering feet on the gravel came back to her. With the sedate pace becoming a young lady, she followed after Minerva and turned down a path that dead-ended in hedge.

She frowned and retraced her steps in another direction.

Over the hedge floated the startled voice of Miss Farnham. "Minerva! Where is Miss Plympton?"

"Lost," said Minerva.

The sounds of Miss Farnham's gentle remonstrances were drowned by Gerard calling, "Evangeline! Where are you?"

What a silly thing to ask, thought Evangeline. How could she know where she was when she was lost? "I am somewhere near the heart of the maze," she called.

"Stay where you are," Gerard commanded. "We shall come find you."

Evangeline sighed. Lost in a maze. It should have been fun, but, somehow, it was not. How very like this visit, she concluded.

"Call to me," Gerard instructed. His voice sounded closer.

"I am here," she replied in dull tones.

"I think I know where you are now," Gerard called back. "We shall be with you in a trice."

The crunch of gravel became louder. Another moment and Gerard and Miss Farnham made their appearance, both looking properly concerned, Miss Farnham towing a reluctant Minerva behind her.

"Now, Minerva," said Miss Farnham, putting her hands on Minerva's shoulders, "you must apologize to Miss Plympton."

"I am sorry," said Minerva in tones that told how very sorry she wasn't.

Evangeline nodded her acceptance. "It was a very clever trick," she added.

Minerva lifted her chin, and for a moment the two regarded each other as enemy generals, each appreciating the other's strength. Then Minerva squirmed out from under Miss Farnham's hands. "Please excuse me," she said and made her escape.

"Oh, dear," fretted Miss Farnham. "I do apologize, Miss Plympton. I cannot understand why she seems to have taken you in such dislike."

"For something to do, I suppose," said Gerard. "Obviously, she is amusing herself by pretending Evangeline is some sort of wicked person. She will have to be punished."

"I shall speak to her," Miss Farnham promised.

"Please, don't worry about it," begged Evangeline. "To continue scolding her can only make her dislike me more."

"Nonsense," said Gerard. "She must learn that one cannot go about imagining every person one encounters to be a villain."

Evangeline wanted to reply that there was nothing wrong with being suspicious of strangers, that sometimes the most ordinary-appearing people turn out to be villains. But she kept silent, refusing to be tricked into betraying her knowledge of the Bane family's perfidy.

At dinner that night, however, Lady Bane's

announcement of her intention to host a dinner in Evangeline's honor caused Evangeline to question her own sound judgment. Was it possible? Had she, perhaps, jumped to conclusions, given a sinister interpretation to actions that were merely high-handed?

No! Do not allow yourself to be lulled into complacency, she cautioned herself. Pretend ignorance, but be ever alert. She looked at Her Ladyship with feigned trust.

"We shall have to invite those silly Amberquail sisters and their mother, I suppose," said Lady Bane. "And the Quinns, the squire and his wife. I believe Lord and Lady Manfred are now at Manfred Park. Perhaps they may be persuaded to join us. . . ."

As Her Ladyship continued to tick off the names of potential guests, Evangeline temporarily lost sight of her determination to be wary, blinded as she was by glorious visions of her first real party.

With a dinner to look forward to, she scarcely noticed the rain, which kept her indoors the next two days. There had been much to do. Helping Lady Bane with the invitations had taken the better part of one morning. And when those were done, Lady Bane had produced an altar cloth and suggested in terms which brooked no refusal that Evangeline might wish to help embroider it. Gerard had liberated the slave by taking her away and teaching her how to play billiards.

After an afternoon spent with him at the billiard table, Evangeline had been forced to admit that he wasn't such a bad sort, really. He still seemed to hold himself aloof, but it had been kind of him to offer to teach her to play the game, at any rate, and he had been remarkably patient with her, considering the fact that she showed little aptitude for it.

In spite of the many activities her cousins found to amuse her, company was sadly lacking. Compared to what she'd imagined the great house would be like, with friends and relatives constantly coming to visit, Deerfield Hall seemed unnaturally quiet and dreary.

By the morning of her third day indoors, Evangeline was feeling restless and fretful. It seemed odd to her that she had heard nothing from her new friend. Had Charlotte tried to contact her? Perhaps she had sent a note and it had been confiscated. Evangeline sat at her dressing table and watched in the looking glass while Smith wound a ribbon through her hair, wondering why they were going to so much bother with her toilette when she would be seeing no one but her gaolers all day.

She went into the drawing room, knowing Lady Bane would soon find her and drag her off to help with the altar cloth again, and as Evangeline was a poor needlewoman, the knowledge did little to cheer her. But the sight that met her eyes cheered her instantly and made her glad she had allowed

Smith to fuss over her hair. "Mr. Hale," she managed.

"Ah, Evangeline," said Lady Bane from the sofa. "I was about to send Joseph to fetch you. As you can see, we have a caller."

Edwin rose and came to bow over Evangeline's hand. She seated herself next to Lady Bane on the sofa, and he resumed his seat. "My sister has come down with a cold and has been confined to her bed these past two days," Edwin informed Evangeline. "She remembered you had promised her a book, *The Captive* . . . ?" He held out his hands and shook his head. "I am afraid the title escapes me, but I am sure you know to which book I refer."

She certainly did! Here was her opportunity. She would write a note to Charlotte asking help (as soon as Charlotte was feeling better) and smuggle the note to her in the book. "Of course," she murmured. "*The Captive Bride*. I shall fetch it immediately."

"There is no need for you to disturb yourself," said Lady Bane. "I shall send Joseph."

"But I am not sure where I laid it," said Evangeline.

"It is, most likely, on your bedside table," said Her Ladyship, undisturbed. "I am sure your abigail will have no trouble finding it. Ring the bellpull, my dear." Lady Bane returned her attention to Edwin. "I do hope, Mr. Hale, you and your papa escape this cold your sister has contracted. Summer colds can run through a family at an alarmingly fast rate."

Trapped, thought Evangeline miserably as Her Ladyship expounded on a variety of cures. The servant appeared and was sent off to fetch the book, and Evangeline sat silent, wondering how she could possibly get a message to Charlotte now.

Ten minutes later Joseph returned, book in hand. "Ah," said Lady Bane. "I see you had no trouble finding the book."

"Smith found it, Your Ladyship," said Joseph. "It was as Your Ladyship said, on the night table."

Lady Bane nodded knowingly.

"I shall just write a quick note to Charlotte," said Evangeline, taking the proferred volume.

"As you wish," said Her Ladyship. "There is writing material in that desk."

She pointed to a corner of the room, and Evangeline hurried over to it, trying to think how to send a message that would have special meaning for her friend, yet give away nothing to Lady Bane should she peruse it. She picked up quill and paper and wrote,

My dear friend,

I am so sorry to hear you are unwell. I hope this book will bear you company. As you read it, think of me.

Yours faithfully . . .

There, thought Evangeline as she signed her name, that should do. Charlotte was well read. She would surely see the hidden meaning in her friend's message.

She handed the book to Mr. Hale. Their hands touched, causing a flutter deep inside Evangeline's chest. He was looking at her so tenderly. What would it feel like if he took her in his arms? She blushed at the boldness of her thought and lowered her eyes.

"I know my sister will be grateful to you for rescuing her from the boredom of the sickroom," he said.

And I hope you both may soon rescue me, thought Evangeline.

The following day was Sunday, and Evangeline found herself more excited to attend church than she'd ever been, knowing it would get her out and away from Deerfield Hall.

As the family took their seats in the same pew where Banes had sat for generations, she stole a quick look around her. She caught sight of the two Hale men, but Charlotte was not with them. Still recovering from her cold, decided Evangeline, and hoped Charlotte wouldn't contract an inflammation of the lungs and go into a decline when her friend so desperately needed her.

A soft thud, followed by a whispered, "Gracious!" and a rustle of silks interrupted Evangeline's thoughts, and she peeped over her shoulder to see a thin woman retrieving her reticule from the aisle before slipping into the pew. Although she was stooped and ready to slide into her seat, Evangeline could tell she was quite tall, as was the slightly plumper female following her in. Both had looked to be in their middle twenties; decidedly on the shelf.

"The Amberquails," announced Lady Bane, still looking straight ahead.

Amazing, thought Evangeline. How had Her Ladyship known without so much as turning about?

The service began and Evangeline made a valiant effort to turn her attention to more holy matters. She at least looked devout, keeping her eyes fixed on the rector during his entire sermon, but her mind raced everywhere but where the rector led. Had Charlotte read her book? Would she have an opportunity before they left the church to meet some of the people Lady Bane had invited to dinner?

As the family made their way out of the church at the end of the service, it appeared Evangeline would, indeed, meet some of the local upper class. The same woman who had dropped her reticule before the service came tripping (literally, for her large feet seemed determined to catch on the hem of her gown) over to the Banes. Her sister, and a middle-aged woman, who Evangeline decided must be the mother, followed at a more sedate pace. The large woman dropped a haphazard curtsy to

Lady Bane. "Your Ladyship. Lord Bane. So good to see you this morning. And this must be your cousin, about whom we have heard so much."

"This is Miss Plympton," said Lady Bane. "Evangeline, my dear, allow me to present you to the Amberquails. . . ."

The tall, clumsy woman was Arabella. Her sister, Fredericka, Evangeline decided, wasn't so pitifully plain. Her plumper lines made her more appealing, and she did have nice brown eyes. Evangeline thought of a cow and suddenly wondered which Amberquail sister had been rescued from the bull by Mr. Hale. As she said all that was proper to the plump Mrs. Amberquail, Evangeline surreptitiously searched for him.

She did not have to search far, for she had barely finished speaking to Mrs. Amberquail when he appeared at her elbow.

"Oh, here is our brave Mr. Hale," gushed Mrs. Amberquail. "To this day I cannot look at a bull without shuddering. Mr. Hale saved my poor Arabella from being gored by a bull," she informed Evangeline. "She was taking a shortcut through Potters' field and not paying the least attention— but that is Arabella through and through, always with her head in the clouds."

Gerard, who had been standing next to Mrs. Amberquail, bit his lip, and Edwin coughed.

Mrs. Amberquail continued, unaware of her witticism, "Mr. Hale is quite the bravest man we know. He scooped my daughter up and ran with her to safety."

Miss Arabella Amberquail was a full head taller than Mr. Hale, and Evangeline found it difficult to imagine him scooping her up and running with her in his arms. So she substituted an image of him running with someone a little smaller, a little lighter, someone with golden curls and blue eyes. She blushed.

Edwin, himself, was looking a little red-faced. "I cannot take credit for rescuing your daughter single-handedly, madam," he told Mrs. Amberquail. "As you know, Mr. Bane was also present, and, fortunately, I was able to hand your daughter over the fence to him and escape, myself. If he had not been present, I am afraid we both would have suffered some severe wounds."

Evangeline looked at her cousin in surprise. He had never mentioned himself when he spoke of Miss Amberquail's rescue. Somehow, it didn't fit with her image of him as a villain.

"Well, Mrs. Amberquail, we shall bid you good day," said the baron. And, in a lowered voice, added to his wife, "Come, Augusta, let us not be standing about yammering all day."

As the Banes settled into their carriage, Evangeline turned to Gerard. "When you told me about Mr. Hale rescuing Miss Amberquail, you neglected to mention your part in the rescue."

Gerard's swarthy face darkened. "It is because I had no real part in it. Hale and I were out riding one day when we happened to see Miss Amberquail strolling through a nearby field, oblivious to a bull on the other side. The bull, on the other hand, was not oblivious to her.

"Hale let out a whoop, spurred his horse, and jumped the fence. Miss Amberquail had seen the bull by then and begun to run. She managed to trip, scare Hale's horse, and unseat him. That was when he . . ." Here Gerard's sober face cracked into a smile. He shook his head. "Oh, my." He sighed, as if trying to regain his composure.

"I don't see what is so funny, Gerard," said his mother sternly.

"I am sorry, Mother. It is just that Hale hardly scooped the lady up and ran with her in the poetic fashion her fond mama describes. He literally dragged her across the field. When he got to the fence, he heaved her at me. She was half scrambling over the thing to begin with, and the gallant rescue ended in all three of us landing in a heap on the other side of the fence."

Evangeline giggled.

"Gerard likes to make light of the incident," said Lady Bane, "but the truth is, that if he and Mr. Hale hadn't happened along, Miss Amberquail would have been gored to death. Mr. Hale may be friendly to a fault, but his bravery can never be questioned. Nor can yours, Gerard," she added generously.

"I am afraid I am not as nobly inclined as Edwin Hale," said Gerard.

"Nonsense," snapped his mother.

He shrugged and the subject was dropped.

The rest of Sunday was a quiet day, as was Monday. By Tuesday Evangeline was counting the hours until Deerfield Hall would ring with the laughter of company. She could hardly wait to see someone besides the Banes.

Tuesday afternoon a servant arrived bearing a message from Charlotte; she sent her regrets that, although much better, she was not yet quite up to going out. Her father felt the necessity of staying home to keep her company, but Edwin would come to represent the family.

While Evangeline had been disappointed to hear Charlotte wouldn't be present, she was elated to hear her brother was still coming. Perhaps he would take her for a walk in the garden. Would a moonlit garden make Mr. Hale so bold as to kiss her? She hoped so.

Wednesday morning Lady Bane did not appear at the breakfast table. "Mother is not feeling too well," said Gerard. "She is keeping to her bed in the hopes that she will feel better this afternoon and not have to cancel the dinner party."

"Oh, dear, I do hope she feels better," said Evangeline. Then, realizing how selfish she sounded, amended, "Not just because of the party, you understand . . ."

Gerard assured her that he understood and left her to entertain herself as best she could.

She sighed. It seemed highly unlikely that Lady

Bane would recover by evening. All for naught, all that work addressing invitations, all that talk, getting her hopes up . . .

But, of course! That was what it had been, simply talk to make her believe she was a guest rather than a prisoner. Lady Bane had never intended to go through with the dinner party. It had all been a hoax, a cruel hoax!

Evangeline's lower lip trembled, and a tear spilled from the corner of first one blue eye, then the other. Fearful that someone would see her crying, she made her escape to the gardens and spent the better part of the morning letting her tears fall into the fish pond.

By afternoon Lady Bane was no better, and servants were dispatched with the bad news— the dinner party would not take place. Neither would Evangeline's romantic stroll in the gardens with Mr. Hale. And, worst of all, freedom from her captors was no closer.

Chapter
5

Dinner that night was a torturous affair. Gerard tried to include Evangeline in the conversation— yet one more attempt to delude her into thinking she wasn't a prisoner. But she was not deluded, not for a moment. Deerfield Hall was like a giant spiderweb, waiting to catch some rich victim in its crumbling threads. And here she was, caught and held by those threads which none could see. There should have been smiling faces all around her this night. Instead, here she was, alone with her captors. She bit her lip in an effort not to cry.

"Curst awkward without Augusta at table," muttered Lord Bane.

Evangeline said nothing.

Dinner finally ended, and she withdrew in solitary state to the drawing room while the men enjoyed their after-dinner wine. The drawing room seemed large and cold without company, but Evangeline decided she preferred her solitude to the company of the Bane men. How she could spend another two hours with them, she didn't know. Evangeline had never been one to feign illness, but now she decided would be a good time to begin. She was sure she felt a headache coming on.

The gentlemen didn't linger over their wine. Too soon they entered the room, and Gerard smiled at her. What a malevolent, gloating smile! Now they thought they had her in their power, but they didn't. They would never succeed with their despicable plans!

"Well, Cousin," said Gerard. "What would you like to do tonight?"

"I should like to retire to my room," said Evangeline. "I am afraid my head is hurting something fierce."

"Most likely you are coming down with the same thing as Augusta," said Lord Bane. He shook his head in disgust. "The place is becoming a demmed pest house."

Feeling chastised, Evangeline made good her escape.

"Does our cousin seem rather skittish to you?" asked Gerard after she had gone.

Lord Bane shrugged. "No more than most females that age. You would never believe what a quiet little thing your mother was when I first met her."

"You are right," said Gerard. "I would not."

Lord Bane gave a snort. "They all change once you marry 'em. So it really doesn't matter whom you marry."

Gerard frowned.

"That is not to say you must marry the chit," added his father hastily. "If she doesn't suit you, then we shall come about one way or the other. But it would put an end to our troubles if she were to have you."

Gerard sighed. "And so it has been for generations."

"The Banes are gamblers," said His Lordship. "Either the tables or the 'change gets us all sooner or later. God knows your grandfather did his share to try and ruin us."

"And I must do my share to try and bring us about," muttered Gerard. He frowned. "I don't think she likes me."

"Nonsense," said Lord Bane. "What is there not to like?"

Gerard shook his head. "Perhaps she senses my lack of enthusiasm."

"Females are funny that way," agreed his father. "Picquet?"

"Why not?"

The two men settled down to play cards and forgot about their cousin, who now paced her bedroom, contemplating her sad fate.

*　　*　　*

The following morning Evangeline was deep
inside the maze, trying to distract herself from
her troubles by learning its secret, when she
heard Gerard call her name. She had no desire to
be cloistered among the tall hedges with her
wicked cousin. She wedged herself into a corner
and remained silent. The crunch of gravel became
louder as Gerard got closer to where she stood,
and Evangeline held her breath and wished she
could as easily stop her noisy heart from beating.
He would be upon her in a moment. She looked at
the walkway and thought of flight. Alas, he would
hear her footsteps on the gravel. She bit her lip
and pressed against the hedge.

Gerard came into sight. "There you are," he
observed. He shot up a questioning eyebrow as
she stepped back onto the path. "Why did you not
answer when I called?"

Evangeline tried to look nonchalant. "Oh, did
you call my name?" she asked. "I did not hear
you."

Now both eyebrows went up.

"I was deep in thought," she added.

"Ah." He nodded his understanding. "May I
bear you company?"

"Of course," said Evangeline, trying to sound
calm. Gerard offered her his arm, and she forced
herself to lay her hand on it.

"And what were you thinking?" he asked.

"Oh, I don't remember," she said airily.

"Perhaps you were thinking of your future," he prompted.

She had, indeed, been thinking of her future and how very grim it looked. "My future?" she hedged.

"And whom you shall marry?" he continued.

"Oh, I am sure I shall not marry for a very long time," said Evangeline.

"Whyever not?"

"Because I shan't marry except for love."

"Very noble sentiments," approved Gerard. "Would that we all could afford to be so noble." He smiled at her. "And if you were to fall in love, what kind of man should you choose?"

"How can I answer such a question?" replied Evangeline. "For how can one know whom one will love?"

Gerard smiled teasingly at her. "It is only a game, Cousin. I beg you not to be so earnest."

Evangeline blushed. "It is a very silly game," she said uneasily.

"Ah, but silly games are the only kind of games played in polite society," said Gerard. "Come now, everyone has preferences. We shall try to discover yours."

"Very well," said Evangeline, trying to sound obliging. After all, there was no sense in angering her cousin. Who knew what he would do to her if he were to become angry? Oh, how she wished she weren't walking in this maze with her hand on his arm!

"Now," said Gerard. "Let us start with character. I suppose, as you are very fond of novels, you would want a man who is noble."

"Oh, yes," agreed Evangeline.

"And brave. Like"—Gerard cocked his head, considering—"Mr. Edwin Hale?"

Evangeline blushed. "Brave, yes," she said.

"Um-hmm," said her cousin, sounding like a physician making his examination. "And now, as to appearance. What sort of coloring do you prefer in a man?"

"Oh, I don't know," said Evangeline evasively, and then, "Are you sure this sort of conversation is proper?"

"Oh, very," Gerard assured her. "Now, as to appearance, do you prefer a man of swarthy complexion, or a man of fair?"

"Fair, I suppose," said Evangeline, seeing Edwin Hale's freckled countenance.

Gerard nodded. "Just as I would have guessed. And what of your papa, Little Cousin? Would he wish you to marry to benefit your family?"

"Papa would want me to be happy, first and foremost," said Evangeline firmly.

"Fortunate creature," murmured Gerard.

Intrigued, Evangeline scrutinized him. "Would not your parents wish the same for you?" she asked.

"For the Banes, duty to family must come before personal happiness," said Gerard. He smiled at Evangeline—a smile lacking warmth—and covered her hand with his. "But sometimes duty can be combined with pleasure." Evangeline snatched her hand from his arm and moved away from him. Now she could see his smile was warmed by genuine amusement. "Do I make you nervous, Little Cousin?" he asked.

"Nervous?" she repeated. "Why should you think that?"

"You seem nervous," he said and took a step closer to her.

"Oh, no, I am not in the least nervous," she stammered in what she hoped was an airy voice. Gerard took a step closer. "That is, I . . ." Evangeline gave up all pretense, picked up her skirt, and ran.

"Evangeline," Gerard half called, half laughed her name and she could hear his feet crunch on the gravel in slow pursuit after her.

She picked up speed and dashed down first one walk, then another. Before she knew it, she was lost.

"Are you lost?" came her cousin's voice from over the hedges.

She made no reply, only ran madly down yet another avenue. Too late, she heard the footsteps. Before she knew it, she had collided with a hard male chest. Strong hands grabbed her arms, and she let out a screech.

"Miss Plympton," said Edwin Hale, searching her face. "Are you all right? I didn't mean to frighten you."

"Mr. Hale," breathed Evangeline. She closed her eyes in relief and let herself go limp in his arms. "I am so very glad to see you."

Gerard had now reached them. "Hale," he saluted his friend. "This is a surprise."

"A not unpleasant one, I hope," said Edwin, his look a question.

"Not at all," said Gerard, smiling and taking Edwin's hand in a firm clasp. "What brings you to the Hall?"

"Once again, I come on an errand for my sister," said Edwin.

"She has taken a turn for the worse?" guessed Evangeline, alarmed.

"No, no," Edwin assured her. "She is recovered and anxious to resume her social life. Which brings me to why she has sent me. Charlotte wishes to celebrate the fact that the weather has finally decided to agree with the calendar. She plans a picnic for tomorrow. She has invited the Amberquails, and is hoping she can prevail on both of you to come as well."

Evangeline clapped her hands together. "How delightful!"

"It would appear we would be delighted to come," said Gerard. "Why don't you walk back to the house and take some sherry, and you can give us further details."

Back at the house, sherry was produced for the gentlemen and ratafia for Evangeline. The three were sitting in the drawing room, discussing the proposed outing, when Lady Bane joined them. "Ah, Mr. Hale, what a pleasant surprise," she said. As Edwin bowed over her hand, Evangeline noted the look Her Ladyship gave him showed more irritation than pleasure.

"Mother! I thought you were unwell," said Gerard.

"You know I never remain in bed more than a day when I have a cold, Gerard," said Lady Bane. "Naturally, I am still weak and my nose makes me most uncomfortable. But," she informed the company in general, "one cannot allow minor illnesses to overcome one. Of course, even the strongest of us must succumb for a short period of time. It is unfortunate I was not well enough yesterday to go forward with our dinner for Evangeline."

"These things happen," said Mr. Hale kindly.

"She is becoming a special part of our family, and we are, naturally, most eager to show her off," continued Lady Bane, smiling fondly at Evangeline, who blushed.

The meaning behind her words was not lost on Edwin Hale. His smile faded.

Gerard cleared his throat and announced, "Mr. Hale has come bearing an invitation from his sister for Evangeline and myself."

"A message from your sister?" Lady Bane favored Edwin with a small smile. "I must say, Mr. Hale, you do have my sympathy."

Edwin looked questioningly at his hostess. "I am not sure I understand," he said.

"Why, you poor boy, you must feel quite ragged, being constantly sent here on one errand after another. How very naughty of your sister to treat you like a servant."

Edwin looked a little embarrassed by Her Ladyship's taunt, but rallied quickly. "How can I object to being sent on such a pleasant errand?" he countered with a smile for Evangeline, which made her blush pink with pleasure. "Truth to tell," he continued, "my sister wished to send a servant, but I begged for the honor of bringing the message myself."

Lady Bane frowned.

"Well," said Gerard, breaking the silence. "We shall be happy to meet you at the stream. The same spot where we picnicked this spring?"

Edwin nodded. "Two o'clock," he said, then took his leave.

He had barely made his exit when Lady Bane let out an indignant snort. "That young man makes a nuisance of himself," she muttered.

"He is merely being friendly, Mother," said Gerard.

"People who are insistently friendly show a certain lack," said Lady Bane.

"What do they lack?" asked Gerard, a teasing smile on his face.

His mother gave him a reprimanding look. "Someone so dependent on others for his entertainment obviously lacks the intelligence to entertain himself."

Gerard merely shook his head. "This," he announced, "is where an intelligent man makes his exit."

"Where are you going?" demanded Lady Bane as he headed for the door.

"Why, to entertain myself. I should hate to be thought lacking," said Gerard and vanished.

"Insolent boy," said Her Ladyship, and scowled. Her gaze fell on Evangeline, and she turned up the corners of her mouth. "Gerard does like to tease."

Evangeline felt a sudden, unaccountable need to defend her cousin. "I am sure he meant no harm," she said timidly.

This seemed to be the right thing to say, for Lady Bane positively beamed on her. "I can see you understand your cousin perfectly well," she said. "He is a dear boy, really, and I am glad to see you are both becoming so fond of each other."

The blood drained from Evangeline's face. What had she done! Her impetuous defense of her cousin against his overbearing mother had been entirely misinterpreted. Now Lady Bane was convinced that her prisoner was becoming fond of her son. "I am only fond of Gerard in a friendly sort of way," she managed.

Lady Bane raised her eyebrows at Evangeline. "Why certainly no one would expect you to feel otherwise, my dear. You have only just met, after all." She leaned across the sofa and patted Evangeline's hand. "Now," she said briskly, rising and closing the subject, "I must consult with the housekeeper about some domestic matters. If you become bored, I hope you will feel free to do some stitching on our altar cloth."

Lady Bane left and Evangeline sighed. For a moment she considered stitching "Help me" on the border of the cloth. Unfortunately, she was sure Lady Bane would see such a thing long before the rector. There was the picnic tomorrow. Perhaps then she would have a chance to tell the Hales of her plight.

Edwin Hale arrived home in a thoughtful mood.

"Why so distracted?" asked his sister.

He shook his head. "No reason," he replied lightly.

"You cannot fool me," said Charlotte. "What happened on your visit to the hall? Was not Evangeline happy to see you?"

"The butler directed me to the garden, where I found Miss Plympton playing a game of hide and go seek with her cousin in the maze. Both were polite, but I am not at all sure either she or Bane was glad to see me."

"Oh," said Charlotte slowly. "And you think she is destined to become the next Lady Bane?"

Edwin shrugged, the picture of nonchalance. "It would stand to reason. They are, after all, related. Both families seem to wish the match."

"And how do you know that?" asked Charlotte.

"Her Ladyship as much as told me," replied Edwin in resigned tones.

"Ah." Charlotte nodded. "But do Evangeline and Gerard wish it?" she countered.

"Bane is a handsome fellow," observed Edwin.

"And so is my brother," said Charlotte stoutly.

"My dear sister," said Edwin. "Miss Plympton is a very lovely girl, but it would appear she is spoken for, so there is an end to it."

"Just like that?"

"Just like that."

Charlotte shook her head. "For shame. I had thought you made of sterner stuff. And I had certainly thought you a more intelligent and observant man."

Edwin frowned at his sister. "I thank you kindly," he said.

"It is plain as a pikestaff she is interested in you—and not her cousin."

"I think what you see is colored by your wishes," said Edwin. "Naturally, it would be most agreeable to have your friend married to your brother, but rarely does life so kindly oblige us."

"Oh, Edwin! How can you be so obtuse?" demanded Charlotte, exasperated. "I tell you, Evangeline is developing a tendre for you. And furthermore, she needs you. Something is not right at that house. I would stake my life on it."

Edwin merely shook his head. "I shan't take that wager. The stakes are entirely too high."

"Bah," said Charlotte in disgust.

*   *   *

The following day the only clouds visible in the blue sky were whispy white ones. The temperature was extremely warm, and Evangeline wondered if they could be at all comfortable eating their picnic under such a hot sky.

As if reading her mind, Gerard assured her that the spot where they were headed would be pleasant, and if they felt warm, they could dip their feet in the stream. "If I remember, Hale has a small skiff. He might be persuaded to take you out on the water."

A pleasant vision of herself and Mr. Hale alone in his boat came to Evangeline. There, at last, she could make her whispered confession. Mr. Hale would take her hand and tell her not to fear, that all would be well. Oh, yes! This was going to be a wonderful day.

They arrived at the appointed spot to find the others there before them. As Gerard helped Evangeline down from the carriage, Charlotte sprang up from a large blanket on the ground and came running to throw her arms around her friend. "Oh, how glad I am to see you! It has been so very long."

"An age," agreed Gerard, and she stuck her tongue out at him. "Never mind your cousin," she said, taking Evangeline by the arm. "He is a great tease. Look who I have!" she called merrily to the Amberquail sisters.

Both ladies were effusive in their greetings. Mr.

Hale was his usual handsome, friendly self, and his sister was at her liveliest. It wasn't long before Evangeline forgot her perilous circumstances and began to enjoy herself.

Several hampers of food and china had accompanied the picnickers, and Mr. Hale filled a plate and brought it to Evangeline. She looked at the cold chicken, sweet bread, and cheeses heaped on her plate and exclaimed, "Oh, my! I shall never be able to eat so much. Perhaps you will share it with me?" she added shyly.

"I should be delighted," said Edwin, sitting down next to her on the blanket. "Well, Miss Plympton, what do you think of our Devon countryside?" he asked.

"It is most beautiful," said Evangeline. "Rather like the Garden of Eden, I imagine."

Edwin smiled at this. "You do have quite an imagination, Miss Plympton."

Evangeline blushed prettily. "I suppose I do," she confessed. "But truly, don't you think it must have looked like this, all green and lovely?"

"Yes, I suppose it must," agreed Edwin.

"I could be happy here," she said with a sigh. This statement seemed to sadden Mr. Hale for some reason, and Evangeline wished she hadn't said it.

"I suppose your family and the Banes are close," he said.

"We haven't been for years," admitted Evangeline. "But now Lady Bane wished to make up for the time that was lost."

Mr. Hale appeared as if he were struggling to say something. But at that moment Miss Arabella Amberquail joined them, and whatever the question was, it died on his lips, and Evangeline found herself heartily wishing Miss Amberquail had found some other spot to sit.

It took the picnickers a good hour to consume the feast provided by the cook at Idyllwilde. At last, however, they sat replete, the ladies under their parasols, the gentlemen cool in their shirts and pantaloons, their jackets and waistcoats flung carelessly aside. After some time spent in idle conversation, Edwin offered to take any of the ladies who would fancy it boating on the stream.

His sister declined the offer, but Miss Arabella Amberquail looked at him with admiring eyes and said she would be thrilled.

Edwin turned to Evangeline. "Miss Plympton, would you care to join us? I believe we can easily fit another person."

It was not exactly her and Mr. Hale alone, thought Evangeline, but it would have to do.

The skiff was put into the water, and Edwin got in, ready to give a hand to each lady and get her settled. There was a moment's panic when Miss Amberquail tripped getting into the boat and set it rocking dangerously, but Edwin managed to balance both boat and lady, and Evangeline was then handed in. She felt a little thrill when Edwin took her hand and assisted her to settle herself.

"Ah, how lovely!" declared Miss Amberquail as Edwin propelled them out into the stream. "Oh, and look, a fish!"

"Where?" cried Evangeline.

"There. There he goes!" Miss Amberquail leaned over, pointing.

"I don't see it," said Evangeline.

"Over there," said Miss Amberquail. She hoisted herself up from her seat, put a steadying hand on Evangeline's shoulder, and leaned off to the side, pointing.

"Miss Amberquail, I beg you not to lean so far out of the boat," cautioned Edwin. "We might . . ."

"Oh!" cried Miss Amberquail, beginning to teeter. She grabbed at Evangeline's shoulder and sat down even as Evangeline jumped up to assist her. Knocked off balance, Evangeline windmilled her arms and fell backward into the stream.

"Evangeline!" screamed Charlotte from the bank, and Gerard plunged into the water.

But Edwin was before him, abandoning ship (and Miss Amberquail) and jumping in to bring up the spluttering gasping Evangeline. "You are quite safe, I assure you," he told her.

But Evangeline couldn't hear him. She was too busy spluttering and crying.

"There now," he murmured, stroking her hair.

Gerard joined him. "Here, Hale, give her to me," he commanded. "While I get her to dry land, I suggest you recover Miss Amberquail before she drifts downstream and out to sea."

Edwin recovered himself, and with a startled "Oh!" waded off in pursuit of the drifting skiff and a very nervous Miss Amberquail.

Evangeline was handed from one rescuer to the other, still carrying on.

"Do stop," commanded her cousin. "You are only waist deep and you shan't drown."

Evangeline stopped, shocked into silence, and Gerard carried her back to shore, where the others awaited her return from a watery grave.

"Oh, you poor dear!" cried Charlotte as a servant wrapped a blanket about Evangeline. "You scared us half to death. How terrible it must have been."

Evangeline whimpered and nodded.

"She was never in danger," said Gerard. "The water was only waist deep."

"People have drowned in less," said Charlotte, springing to her friend's defense.

Gerard's swarthy cheeks turned a deep mahogany, and both Charlotte and Evangeline's faces went fiery red, as the memory of how Gerard's brother died came to hover over them.

"I had best take you home to change," Gerard said to Evangeline.

"Oh, yes," agree Charlotte earnestly. "Then you may both return. We will all be here for a good long time still."

"I am sure your brother will wish to go home and change," said Gerard stiffly.

"Edwin is very hearty," insisted Charlotte. "He will stay and let the sun dry him." She turned to Evangeline. "Please do return," she begged, including Gerard in her invitation. "It would be a shame to let our day end on such an unpleasant note."

"Come, Cousin," said Gerard. He thanked Charlotte politely for a wonderful time and assisted Evangeline into the carriage.

"You cannot make me remain at the Hall," declared Evangeline as they drove off.

Gerard looked at her, astonished. "No," he agreed, "I cannot."

"You cannot keep me hidden," she continued, her voice tinged with hysteria.

"You are correct on both counts, Cousin," agreed Gerard. "Are you chilled?" he asked solicitously.

Evangeline's teeth were chattering. "I shall be fine," she insisted.

The rest of their drive home was accomplished in silence. Gerard dropped Evangeline at the front porch. She kept her face averted as he helped her alight, and the minute he released her, she fled. He drove on to the stables and left both horse and carriage in the competent hands of the groom.

He went straight to his room to change, then made his way to his mother's sitting room, where he found Lady Bane busy with her correspondence.

"Gerard. I did not expect you back so soon."

"I did not expect to be back so soon, but Miss Amberquail necessitated an early return."

"Miss Amberquail? Oh, dear."

"Precisely," said Gerard. "Our dear Miss Amberquail managed to pitch Evangeline into the stream."

"What!" declared his startled mother.

"Never fear," said Gerard. "I have rescued the goose that lays the golden eggs."

Lady Bane frowned at her son. "I wish you would not speak in such crass terms," she chided.

"I wish I did not need to speak of the girl at all," retorted Gerard. He began to pace. "A pretty bride you have chosen for me, my dear mother," he said.

"What can you mean?" demanded Her Ladyship.

"I mean that your fine heiress is dicked in the nob."

"Gerard, how can I understand you when you insist on speaking in that detestible cant?"

"I am sorry, Mother. Allow me to make myself plain. Our beautiful cousin, the lady whom you were sure I could have no objections to marrying, is mad as a March hare."

Chapter
6

"Nonsense!" snapped Her Ladyship. "The child is as sane as you or I. Why would you think such a thing?"

"Why, no reason at all," replied her son, flinging out an arm. "It is of no consequence that she became hysterical for no reason and says things that make no sense. I merely stated that she is mad because I thought it an amusing jest. Bah!" He collapsed onto a daintily cushioned chair and sunk his chin into his cravat.

"You must have said something to upset her," said Lady Bane calmly.

"I said nothing," Gerard retorted. "I did nothing—unless you call bringing her home to change out of her wet gown doing something terrible."

"Well, if you talked to her in the impatient way in which you are now speaking to your mama, I can see why she was upset," observed Her Ladyship.

If she sought an apology from her vexed son, she sought in vain. Gerard sat silent, his eyebrows slanted in an angry V.

"You must be more gentle, dearest," Lady Bane continued, following her own advice. "Our cousin is young and inexperienced. Perhaps gentlemen make her nervous." She studied her son. His expression remained unchanged. "I am sure I need not remind you how very much we need the Plympton money."

Gerard slumped down in his chair and deepened his scowl.

"If there were any other way, you know we would take it. But there is no other way. As the only son—"

Gerard cut her off with a wave of his hand. "Yes, I know," he said bitterly. "It is my responsibility to save the family fortunes."

"So it has always been. You are not the only aristocrat to marry beneath him."

"Or without love," added Gerard.

Lady Bane's face showed what she thought of such silly romantic notions. "Young men do not worry about such things when choosing a wife, as I am sure your father has told you."

"I am well aware of how young men are supposed to behave," replied her son stiffly.

Lady Bane tried cajolery. "Is it such a great punishment to marry the girl? She is quite lovely."

"Oh, yes," agreed Gerard. "And any offspring she gives me will be equally so. We shall have the loveliest madhouse in all of Devon." With that he rose and stalked from the room, ignoring his mother's imperious use of his name.

He wandered down to the drawing room to await his cousin in dry clothes. Fifteen minutes passed and he began to pace the room. Another fifteen minutes and Evangeline still made no appearance, asking him to return her to the picnic. He wandered to the French doors and gazed out onto the garden. Catching sight of Miss Farnham and Minerva, the scowl lifted from his face, and he slipped outside.

Minerva was the first to see her brother approach. "Gerard!" she shrieked and ran to him. Catching his hand, she announced, "Miss Farnham and I are about to play hide and go seek. Will you play with us?"

"I am sure your brother has more important things on his mind than to play hide and go seek," said Miss Farnham, blushing.

"Not at all," Gerard assured her. To his sister, he said, "You go hide and I shall come seek you."

Minerva clapped her hands. "Close your eyes," she commanded. Gerard obeyed. "Now count to ten very slowly."

"One," said Gerard, and Minerva dashed off. He opened his eyes and caught Miss Farnham's arm as she moved away. "Two," he called, watching Minerva disappear behind the hedges of the maze. "Three. Walk with me," he begged Miss Farnham in a low voice, offering his arm. Her face a glowing pink, she took it as he called, "Four," and led her away in the opposite direction.

Evangeline came downstairs. She saw no sign of her cousin waiting in the hallway to return her to the picnic. She made her way to the drawing room. The French doors stood ajar. She went to them and looked outside but saw no one. Gerard had made himself scarce. He obviously had no intention of taking her back to the picnic.

Her lips trembled and a tear slipped out the corner of her eye. It was as she'd known all along. In spite of the doors left deceptively ajar, she was a prisoner in this place. "Oh, Mr. Hale," she sobbed. "Rescue me."

The prisoner spent the remainder of the day cloistered in her room. When she made her appearance at dinner that night, her eyes were bloodshot and her nose red. She kept her gaze on her plate and replied in monosyllables to her hostess's questions about the picnic.

Lady Bane was unaffected by this show of misery. In fact, she seemed not to notice it. "I have rescheduled our dinner party," she announced.

Evangeline could hardly believe her ears. So she was not to be kept isolated after all! "How wonderful!" she exclaimed, dejection abandoned. "When shall you have it?"

Lady Bane smiled at Evangeline and said, "The end of the week. We shall have no trouble getting our neighbors to come on such short notice, I am sure. It is no small thing to be invited to a dinner at Deerfield Hall, and they have, most likely, all been waiting anxiously for us to reschedule the affair."

Evangeline heard none of this speech. She was busy envisioning herself and Mr. Hale in the drawing room, standing away from the other guests, talking earnestly. He took her hand and kissed it . . .

"Does that sound agreeable to you?" Lady Bane repeated herself.

Evangeline smiled. "Oh, yes," she breathed.

Evangeline worried that, perhaps, she would take cold after her fall in the stream, but no such unhappy circumstance occurred, and the day of the dinner party arrived with no obstacles presenting themselves to halt the event.

"So very good of Your Ladyship to invite us," gushed Mrs. Amberquail as the guests mingled about the drawing room, awaiting their summons to the dining table. "It is always a pleasure to be at Deerfield Hall."

"And it is always a pleasure to receive our neighbors," replied Lady Bane with a condescending nod.

Evangeline stood next to Her Ladyship, surveying the guests. In addition to the Amberquails, the squire and his wife and son were present, as well as the Quinns and their celebrated daughter, recently returned from a house party at the home of her betrothed. Miss Quinn was lovely in a pale green gown that showed off her creamy skin and auburn curls. The squire's son, a thick young man, stood earnestly talking with the beauty. Evangeline watched him strain to keep his chin above his shirt points, and thought of a turtle pushing its head outside its shell.

Unlike her earlier vision, Mr. Hale stood across the room, far removed from her, visiting with Gerard. But he stole frequent glances in Evangeline's direction, which she found nearly as satisfying as having him at her side.

Grimley made his appearance and intoned that dinner was served. Lady Bane led the way in to the dining room on the arm of the squire, the highest-ranking guest, while her husband did his duty by the squire's wife, the rest following them.

Evangeline was, to her regret, seated next to her handsome cousin, and Mr. Hale, she noted was placed as far from her as possible. Ah, well, perhaps after dinner they would have a chance to converse.

Miss Arabella Amberquail sat on her other side and lost no time in apologizing, yet again, for her part in Evangeline's unfortunate dunking in the stream. Miss Amberquail sighed. "How fortunate that Mr. Hale was on hand to rescue you." Here she stole a glance at Mr. Hale, and her long face took on a rosy hue. "I do believe he is looking at us."

Evangeline cast her glance across the table and caught Mr. Hale's eyes on her. She felt her face grow warm, but she managed to give him a timid smile, which he returned, if a little wistfully.

Miss Amberquail was smiling, too. She lowered her voice. "Ever since he rescued me from that crazed bull, he has watched over me most assiduously."

"He is very chivalrous," agreed Evangeline.

"Oh, it is more than that, I am sure." Now Miss Amberquail's face was a very deep pink. "That is, well . . ."

She tittered nervously, and Evangeline's eyes widened. "Why, Miss Amberquail, do you think Mr. Hale is interested in you?"

Miss Amberquail stole a peek at Mr. Hale. "Oh, no," she said modestly. "I am sure it is, as you say, that he is just chivalrous."

But Evangeline could tell Miss Amberquail thought nothing of the sort. Again, she looked across the table at Mr. Hale, who was now conversing with Lord Bane. She had been sure Mr. Hale was interested in her. And it hardly suited her romantic notions to have him anxious to be chivalrous to any lady other than herself.

Perhaps Mr. Hale wasn't interested in her. He had made no effort to come to her side before dinner. Suddenly the turtle soup in Evangeline's stomach felt very heavy, and her future looked very bleak. Who else could she turn to in her hour of need save Mr. Hale? She knew of no other man in the entire world who had the same qualifications to be a proper hero. And there was certainly no other man with whom she would rather ride off into the dark and stormy night on a white horse. Evangeline laid down her spoon. Thus far, the dinner party she had so long awaited was turning out to be a sad disappointment.

Dinner ended, and the ladies left the gentlemen to their port and repaired to the drawing room. Miss Quinn, giving Evangeline an assessing look, took a seat opposite her, while Charlotte took one next to her.

"It is nice to have you back among us," Charlotte said politely to Miss Quinn. "How did you find the Marquess of Winston's family home?"

"Quite nice," said Miss Quinn in a haughty voice. "His estate is large, and the house is very lovely. I shall, of course, redecorate. The furniture is old, and I prefer the Grecian style."

"Naturally," murmured Charlotte. "I am sure you will be very happy."

"It will suit me," said Miss Quinn.

It? thought Evangeline. Miss Quinn refers to her husband as if he were some sort of object? "The marquess is a wonderful man, I am sure," she ventured.

Miss Quinn looked at Evangeline as if she were

odd. "He will do," she said, effectively silencing Evangeline and causing her to wonder if no one other than her parents ever thought of marrying for affection rather than gain.

"Speaking of brides," said Charlotte, turning to Evangeline, "I keep forgetting to tell you, I finished *The Captive Bride* when I was ill and found it the most wonderful compensation for lying sick abed. That poor girl." Charlotte shook her head.

Evangeline's heart thumped excitedly, urging her to take advantage of the opportunity before her. She opened her mouth to speak, but Charlotte rushed on.

"Of course, I know I should have returned it by now. I had it in the carriage to give to you at the picnic and then quite forgot until after you left. I kept hoping you would return."

"I wanted to," said Evangeline, "but Gerard would not bring me back."

Charlotte frowned. "It is too bad of him, really," she said. "I shall have to scold him."

"Charlotte," began Evangeline.

Charlotte held up her hand. "I know, I should have brought the book tonight. But I will return it tomorrow when we pay our thank-you call. I promise you, I shan't forget." She then turned to Lady Bane. "Your Ladyship," she chirped, "this is proving a most delightful dinner. And now, you must allow us to reciprocate your hospitality and give a ball in Miss Plympton's honor."

A ball! Images of lobster patties and waltzing

with Mr. Hale sprang to Evangeline's mind, crowding out her worries and making her forget her need to explain to Charlotte why she had leant her a book about an imprisoned heiress.

Miss Fredericka Amberquail clasped her hands together. "Oh, a ball! What a wonderful idea! It has been so long since I danced," she informed the company.

"Now, dearest, it has not been so very long," corrected her mama. "Why, only last summer, in Bath, we attended the subscription balls."

Miss Amberquail's eyes fell. "It has been a long time since I danced," she repeated softly, and sympathetic silence draped the room.

"Well, then," said Charlotte in an attempt to lighten the mood, "let us make sure we remedy that! I shall invite every eligible male from miles around." And here she smiled conspiratorially. "And I shall make sure to invite twice as many gentlemen as ladies," she added.

"An excellent idea," said Miss Fredericka Amberquail.

"I am not sure such a grand affair would be at all the thing," said Lady Bane. "After all, Evangeline is not yet out officially. . . ."

"Oh, but neither am I," said Charlotte. "That is, I have not yet been presented, although I should have been last year. I am sure if we keep it small, and Papa is there, and you and Lord Bane, and just some of our neighbors . . . ?" She looked questioningly at Lady Bane.

"I brought a ball gown," put in Evangeline shyly.

"A ball is such a delightful event," said Mrs. Amberquail. "Just what we need to liven up the summer. Summer can drag on so."

"Well," said Lady Bane stiffly, "I had been considering having a ball at Deerfield Hall—just a small affair."

"Oh, but your ladyship has just held this splendid dinner," protested Charlotte. "To ask you to turn 'round and plan a ball would be positively cruel. And besides," she added with an impish grin, "I have already ordered the flowers."

The other ladies laughed, a sure sign of support, and it appeared that any objections Lady Bane might have were overridden.

At that moment the gentlemen joined them, and Evangeline saw Miss Arabella Amberquail look at Mr. Hale with a speculative gleam in her eye.

But Mr. Hale made a beeline to where Evangeline and his sister sat and took the empty seat next to Evangeline.

"Well, Edwin," said Charlotte. "I have just told the ladies of our intentions to have a ball, and they are all in favor of the idea."

"Excellent," said Edwin heartily. "I hope, Miss Plympton, that you will save me a dance."

"I shall be delighted, sir," she said, demurely lowering her eyes even as her heart skipped and danced like a hoyden.

Gerard, who had followed in on Edwin's heels, said, "And I hope you will also save me one, Cousin."

Evangeline's heart settled back to a more sedate pace. "Of course," she said politely.

"And," added Edwin gallantly, "I know our kind neighbors will save us a dance as well."

Both Amberquail sisters turned pink with pleasure and nodded.

The subject of a ball was finally exhausted, and the company amused themselves the rest of the evening by listening to the Amberquail sisters perform on the pianoforte. Neither sister had been gifted with good looks, but both had some measure of musical talent. So the evening passed pleasantly. And although Edwin's behavior toward Evangeline was that of a polite friend rather than ardent suitor, his very nearness made her feel both happy and nervous at once.

The next day Evangeline had a letter from her papa. "My dear child," she read, "I am happy to hear you are having a splendid time with our relatives. Meanwhile, I console myself with writing to you. This absence, I suppose, is but a foretaste of what your poor papa will suffer once you are happily settled in a home of your own."

Evangeline gulped, envisioning herself forever at Deerfield Hall, seeing Mr. Hale every day but belonging to another, whose family greedily spent her money on their odious mansion.

She read the rest of the letter with a heavy

heart, wishing she were safe back at her dull home with her papa.

With a sigh she laid aside the letter and went outside to settle herself by the fishpond. She idly watched the fat goldfish swim about and saw Edwin Hale's smiling face. If she had not come to Deerfield Hall, perhaps she would never have met Mr. Hale. She closed her eyes and pretended he was sitting next to her. So successfully did her imagination serve her, she could almost feel him next to her.

"Well, Cousin. And how are the fishes today?"

Evangeline jumped at the sound of Gerard's voice and scrambled to her feet. "Good morning," she managed. "I was just enjoying the sunshine."

"And a fine morning for it," he agreed and smiled.

His eyes strayed from her face, to rake lustfully over her no doubt, and with horror Evangeline saw him reach a hand to her shoulder. The beast! He would ravish her here in plain sight of everyone? She let out a gasp and squirmed away, then gave her attacker a mighty push, catching him unaware and toppling him into the fish pond.

Gerard sat up, spluttering and shaking his head. "What the devil—" he began.

Evangeline didn't stay to answer him. Instead, she fled into the house.

Once inside, she was informed by the cadaverish Grimley that the Hales were in the drawing room with Lady Bane. Relief flooded Evangeline.

Sure her thoughts of him had summoned the noble Edwin Hale, she hurried to the drawing room to see him.

The door had been left open in expectation of her arrival, and Lady Bane greeted her as she entered the room. "Ah, Evangeline. Did you enjoy your walk in the garden? And where, pray, is Gerard? I thought he was keeping you company."

"Gerard?" repeated Evangeline, and a guilty flush surfaced on her neck and face. "I am sure he will be in shortly."

Her Ladyship frowned over this unsatisfactory answer and she grabbed the bellpull.

Grimley appeared. "Your Ladyship?"

"See to it my son is informed we have visitors," said Lady Bane.

"It has been done, Your Ladyship," said Grimley. "He has asked me to tell you that he will be with you shortly."

As if on cue, the sound of approaching footsteps drifted into the room. There was something not quite normal about this particular sound. Lady Bane scowled as the *squish-squish* became identifiable as emanating from her son, her very wet son. He slopped by the open door, Edwin and Charlotte watching in amazement, and called, "I shall be with you in a trice."

Lady Bane scowled. As her guests turned their amazed faces her way, she shrugged her shoulders and tried to turn the scowl into a playful smile. "Did some mishap occur in the garden?" she inquired of Evangeline.

Evangeline's face was a glowing red now. "I am afraid so," she said. "Gerard fell into the fish pond."

Her Ladyship shut her eyes and nodded slowly. "I see," she said.

Evangeline doubted the veracity of this statement, but decided she wouldn't be the one to bring sight to the blind.

Grimley arrived with refreshments, and the subject of Gerard's strange behavior was politely left behind.

Gerard joined them ten minutes later, looking none the worse for his morning dunking, announcing to the company in general that he had been assisting Evangeline in counting the fish and had slipped and fallen in.

"How perfectly odious!" exclaimed Charlotte. "I should hate to fall into a fish pond."

"Ah, well," said Gerard. "At least we cannot say our morning has been uneventful, can we, Cousin?"

Evangeline felt the taunt in her cousin's words and lowered her eyes in an effort to escape Lady Bane's disapproving gaze. When at last she raised her eyes, it was to find Charlotte looking questioningly at her. She tried to put all her desperation in the look she returned her friend, and this made Charlotte's brow furrow.

"Well, my dear," said her brother. "We had best

be on our way. I am sure Lady Bane will be busy with other callers throughout the day, and we must not overstay our welcome."

Charlotte recalled herself. "Yes, of course," she said. "We shall take our leave, but not before we obtain a promise from Evangeline that she come take luncheon with us tomorrow. Do say you will." She smiled at Gerard. "And you, too, of course, Mr. Bane," she murmured.

"Oh, yes," said Evangeline quickly. "I should very much like to come."

"And I shall be happy to bring her," said Gerard politely.

The Hales took their leave, and as soon as they were riding down the drive, Charlotte spoke. "Edwin, I am convinced there is something very strange about that household. Did you see the look Evangeline gave me when we took our leave?"

Edwin shrugged, the perfect picture of disinterest. "Perhaps Miss Plympton is homesick."

His sister glared at him in irritation. "Really, Edwin. You never used to be so dull-witted. Something is not right at that house, I tell you. And I intend to find out what it is. I wish you to take Mr. Bane away after we have dined tomorrow so I may have some time alone with Evangeline. Then, perhaps, I may be able to get to the bottom of this."

"Very well," agreed Edwin. "I have been wanting to show that new mare to him. Tomorrow will be as good a time as any."

* * *

Evangeline wasn't thrilled with the prospect of her cousin's company on the ride to Idyllwilde, but once there, she determined to shed him and confess her predicament to Charlotte. Now that Gerard was becoming bolder in his advances, there wasn't a moment to lose.

She chatted determinedly as her cousin tooled his curricle down the road, hoping both to keep him from the subject of their encounter at the fish pond and to distract him from making further advances. Her plan succeeded, and they arrived at their destination with Evangeline's virtue and Gerard's clothes intact.

The Hales greeted them with their customary enthusiasm, and luncheon was an enjoyable meal, seasoned with Charlotte's lively conversation.

After they had eaten and repaired to the drawing room, Edwin turned to Gerard. "How would you like to see that new brood mare of mine?" he offered.

"Very much," replied Gerard.

"I am sure the ladies will excuse us," said Edwin with a smile for his sister. "I know they have been longing to be free of our company this past hour."

"We only wish to be shed of your company if you are going to talk horseflesh," teased Charlotte.

"As that is exactly what we intend to discuss, we shall give you a respite," replied her brother, rising.

The senior Mr. Hale showed no inclination to

leave. Settling into his chair, he turned to Evangeline and said, "And so, Miss Plympton, how have you enjoyed meeting our neighbors?"

Evangeline sighed inwardly. She was anxious to confess her great danger to Charlotte, but hesitated in front of Mr. Hale for fear he wouldn't believe her. "I enjoyed it very much," she answered. "They all seem to be very kind, the sort of people who would never hesitate to help someone in trouble," she ventured to add.

"Oh, yes," agreed Mr. Hale calmly. "A very nice neighborhood. We have been most happy since coming to live here. Most happy." And he proceeded to elucidate.

Meanwhile, the two young men were at the stables examining a fine-looking black mare with bloodlines that Edwin assured his guest were impeccable. "Think what we'd have if we bred her to that stud of mine," said Gerard.

Edwin nodded. "A fine thought," he agreed and gave the horse one final pat before leaving the stall.

Outside the stables, Edwin brought up the subject of Evangeline. "How are you enjoying your cousin's company?" he asked, his voice casual.

Gerard's countenance lost its pleasant cast. "My mother thinks my cousin a most excellent young woman," he said.

"But you don't?"

"She is . . . eccentric."

Edwin's brows lowered. "Eccentric," he repeated,

allowing the full implications of the word to blossom
in his mind. "How did you happen to tumble into
your fish pond yesterday?" he asked suddenly.

"She pushed me," said Gerard simply.

Edwin's eyes widened. "She pushed you! Well,
perhaps you said something."

"I said nothing," protested Gerard. "I merely
tried to remove a spider from her sleeve, and she
let out a squeal and pushed me into the pond."

"It is hard to imagine such a sweet girl doing
something so violent," mused Edwin.

"I am afraid my cousin is given to, er, odd
starts," said Gerard. "This was not the first."

Edwin cocked a disbelieving eyebrow. "Then
you are telling me she is . . . ?"

Gerard bit his lip and nodded.

"What are you telling me?" cried Charlotte,
looking at her friend in amazement. Her father
had finally taken himself off, and now the two
girls sat together on the sofa.

"It is true," said Evangeline, and added in a
tragic voice, "I am an heiress."

"An heiress," breathed Charlotte.

Evangeline nodded. "Just like the poor creature
in the book I loaned you."

Charlotte gasped. *"The Captive Bride?"*

"Charlotte," said Evangeline, grabbing her
friend's hand, "There is something I must tell
you."

But before Evangeline could confess her grave

danger the gentlemen reentered the drawing room.

"Ah," said Edwin amiably, "I can see you have not missed us in the least."

"We certainly have not," said Charlotte, casting her brother a reprimanding look. "I do believe you could have been gone another twenty minutes and we should not have missed you in the least."

Edwin shrugged as if to say, "I did my best."

"Ah, well," continued Charlotte. "Now you have returned, you will just have to listen to us discuss the upcoming ball."

As soon as their guests were gone, Charlotte's carefree smile was replaced by a sober look. "It is as I suspected," she told her brother. "Something is definitely wrong."

"It certainly is," agreed her brother with a sad face.

"And," continued Charlotte, too full of her own news to pay any attention to her brother's drooping countenance, "I have made the most important discovery. Evangeline is—"

"Mad," supplied Edwin with a heavy sigh.

Chapter
7

"Mad!" echoed Charlotte. "What a ridiculous thing to say! Why, she is no more mad than I. What could have given you such a ridiculous idea"

"Not what, but whom," corrected Edwin. "Bane told me just now."

Charlotte looked at her brother in disgust. "Did he also tell you that Evangeline is an heiress?"

Edwin's brows knit. "An heiress, you say?"

Charlotte nodded. "Yes," she said. "And I think she is in danger."

"Danger!" echoed Edwin. "She told you that?"

"Well, in so many words," ammended Charlotte. "She told me she was just like the heroine in the book she loaned me. And the heroine in *The Captive Bride*, my dear brother, was an heiress, the same as Evangeline."

"Who was . . . let me guess . . . held captive?" prompted Edwin, openly skeptical.

"*By* her relatives, who wished her to marry the son of the house."

Edwin made a face. "Really now, Charlotte," he said.

"And what, pray, is so preposterous about the idea that Evangeline's relatives mean to force her to marry Gerard?" demanded Charlotte. "Heaven knows, with that crumbling old place they could use the funds."

"Well, yes, but—" began her brother.

"And furthermore, she was about to confess something very important to me just when you two came in. Whose idea was it to leave the stable so soon and come back into the house?" Charlotte demanded.

"Why, no one's."

"Who was the first to leave the stable?"

"Well, Bane, I suppose," said Edwin.

"And why do you suppose he was so anxious to leave the stable and get back to the house?"

"Curse it all, Charlotte! He wasn't anxious. We simply left the stable and came back. Men are not like women. They don't stand about after they are finished with something. They leave."

Charlotte ignored this. "I shall tell you why he was so anxious to return to the house. It was because he feared to leave his cousin alone with me for long. He knew she would confide in me. He knew we would learn of his family's wicked plot. If you had only kept him away a moment longer, I should have known all," she finished, looking accusingly at her brother.

"This is preposterous," objected Edwin. "Whoever heard of such nonsense outside the covers of a book?"

"What of those two little princes who were killed by one of the Richards?" argued his sister.

Edwin rolled his eyes. "We are hardly speaking of the line of succession to the throne of England," he said.

"Why would Evangeline be so upset?" continued Charlotte, ignoring her brother's damping words. "Why would she refer to that book as if it contained vital information?"

"Why, indeed? Unless she is . . ." Edwin bit his lip, and the horrible word remained unspoken.

"I don't believe for a moment that Evangeline is mad," declared Charlotte. "And neither should you."

"Well, I certainly don't wish to," said Edwin hotly.

"I should think not," said Charlotte, looking at him scornfully. "What kind of lover are you, anyway? First you are ready to believe her as good as betrothed to Mr. Bane, and now you wish to think her mad!" At this, Edwin's cheeks turned russet. "You do love her, don't you?" prompted Charlotte gently.

Edwin bit his lip, a miserable look on his face.

"Well, then. Are you simply going to sit by and see her used in such a terrible way?"

Edwin's chin jutted out. "No," he said. "Of course not! If it is really true she is in trouble, naturally I want to help her. Oh, Lord," he moaned, rubbing his forehead. "This tale you tell me is so far-fetched I hardly know what to believe."

"You had best believe your sister," said Charlotte tartly. "I have already told you Evangeline is in trouble. We must stand ready to help her when she needs it, even if it means taking her from that house by force."

The russet hue in Edwin's face faded to ash white.

"If they hold her prisoner there, we shall have to," pointed out Charlotte.

"We will do nothing until we learn whether or not what you have told me is true," said her brother firmly. "I certainly shan't sit by and see Miss Plympton abused in any way, but we cannot go charging into our neighbors' house abducting their house guest simply because one of us suspects something is not quite right."

"I hope you do not live to regret such caution," said Charlotte in a voice of doom.

The prisoner of Deerfield Hall returned to find Lady Bane entertaining the Amberquail ladies. "Oh, how fortunate that we had not yet left!" cried Mrs. Amberquail as Gerard and Evangeline walked into the room. "We were about to take our leave, but it is so pleasant to have the opportunity to see both Mr. Bane and Miss Plympton for a moment before we do so. Is it not, girls?"

Fredericka Amberquail was looking at Gerard as though he were a spun sugar delicacy. If only you knew what a beast he truly is, thought Evangeline as Gerard politely bowed over each of the ladies' hands, you would not look at him so.

"Alas, we cannot stay long," continued Mrs. Amberquail. "We must get home for our rest. I always insist the girls lie down upon their beds for two hours every afternoon," she said, in an aside for anyone interested. "A lady cannot hope to look her finest unless she is well rested at all times." Here Mrs. Amberquail beamed approvingly on Evangeline. "I can see that Miss Plympton takes care to keep well rested. Let that be an example to you, girls. I think sometimes my daughters do not appreciate their mama's advice," she informed the company.

Both daughters were blushing now, and Lady Bane added her own advice, "Rest and exercise, both are necessary for the constitution. That has always been my secret."

"Oh, yes," agreed the plump Mrs. Amberquail. "A nice stroll now and then is very beneficial. Now, girls, I think we should be on our way. Dear Lady Bane, we thank you again for a most delightful evening. We should have been here yesterday," she explained to Evangeline, "but poor Fredericka was feeling quite done up. Rich food does not agree with her, don't you know. Nonetheless, it was a delightful evening. I cannot remember when I have enjoyed myself more. Well, now, girls, we must stop dawdling and be on our way. I am sure such an important woman as Lady Bane has other things to do besides sit all day and listen to us rattle on. Come along, now."

After a few more references to taking her leave, Mrs. Amberquail finally made good on her promise, and Gerard heaved a sigh. "That woman is exhausting," he said.

"It is her two hours of daily rest that gives her so much energy," said Lady Bane acerbically. She turned her attention to Evangeline. "And how did you find our neighbors, the Hales?"

"Very well," said Evangeline.

Lady Bane smiled her drooping, sinister smile at Evangeline. "I am so glad you have found a friend your age in the neighborhood," she said. "The Hales are quite nice. A pity the poor man has no title. It leaves his son with little to interest a lady of marriageable age."

Evangeline conjured up Edwin Hale's strong shoulders and kind smile and thought that Mr. Hale had quite a bit to recommend him to a lady.

"He is not without fortune," said Gerard.

"Fortune. What is that compared to a title?" scoffed Her Ladyship. "Isn't that right, Evangeline?"

Evangeline found both mother and son looking at her with interest. She knew the answer they wanted. "I suppose a title is a nice thing to have," she managed.

"It most certainly is," said Lady Bane with a vigorous nod of the head. "A man who bears a title is a man whose background speaks of integrity, a man whose family has proved their superiority."

"And therefore need no longer evidence either in his own life," added her son casually.

"Gerard!"

Gerard refused to look chastised. "Mama?"

"How can you say such a thing?"

"Why, quite easily, I am afraid. I have only to think of some of the fine specimens I see in the ton; rakes and gamblers, unethical sellers of privilege." He turned to Evangeline. "You would do better to marry before you ever go out in society, Cousin, for you don't know what wickedness disguised in a title and fancy ball attire may offer for you."

Lady Bane looked thoughtful. "Gerard is correct," she said to Evangeline. "It is hard for a young lady with no experience of society to know who can and cannot be trusted, who is a good catch and who is not. Better to marry someone whose family one knows."

Evangeline was feeling increasingly nervous with the direction the conversation was taking. If she remained in the room much longer, Gerard would offer for her then and there, and before she knew it, Lady Bane would be writing to tell her papa she was engaged. "I am sure that is very good advice," she said meekly. "If you will excuse me, I think, perhaps, I shall follow Mrs. Amberquail's advice and go to my room for a rest."

Lady Bane was all concern. "Certainly, dear. An excellent idea. You are looking a trifle peaked." Evangeline scuttled out of the room, and Lady Bane turned an approving smile on her son. "That was most brilliant," she said as soon as Evangeline had gone.

Gerard scowled. "I should hate you to labor under the mistaken belief that I was being brilliant on behalf of your plan to marry me to the girl. I merely felt it fair to warn her."

"And a wise warning it was," agreed his mama. "She will certainly appreciate your offer all the more when it comes."

For a moment Gerard looked as if he might say something, but with a shake of the head merely left the room.

Lady Bane shook her head and took up her needlework.

Abovestairs, Evangeline allowed Smith to help her out of her gown. "Are you feeling quite all right, miss?" ventured Smith.

A ragged sigh escaped Evangeline's lips. "I am most miserable," she confessed.

"With such lovely gowns, and being so pretty, and staying at such a wonderful old house as this?" Smith's voice held awe and disbelief. "Why, only look at this gown," she said, holding up the delicate muslin concoction. "What I wouldn't give to own such a fine gown."

Evangeline was momentarily distracted from her own troubles. "And what would you do with such a fine gown, Smith?" she asked.

"Oh, I would wear it on my free Sunday afternoon. The new footman, George, would see me in it, and say, 'And where did you get such a fine gown, Smith?' And I would reply, 'Oh, la! This old thing? I have had it an age.' And he would say, 'You look ever so nice in it. Just like a fine lady.' Then he would ask me if I would like to go walking with him. And I would tell him yes, and as we were out walking, everyone would see me in my fine gown and think I was a real lady." Smith ended her soliloquy with a sigh.

"Well, then," said Evangeline. "I wish you would take it."

"I beg your pardon, miss?" said Smith, dazed.

"Please take it," urged Evangeline. "It is really my least favorite gown, and I was thinking of getting rid of it."

"Oh, heavens!" gasped Smith. "Just getting rid of it? Such a beautiful gown?"

"I think it would look very nice on you," said Evangeline.

"Oh, thank you, miss," breathed Smith, hugging the gown to her. "I shall have to let it out a little in the bodice, but I think the skirt length will be just right. Oh, thank you!"

Evangeline smiled. "Think nothing of it. It is

certainly no less than you deserve. You have been so good to me. And so loyal. You would be loyal to me, would you not?" she asked, suddenly inspired.

Smith looked surprised. "Well, I should hope so. I'm sure I have always given satisfaction."

"If your mistress were in danger, would you help her?"

Smith's eyes grew wide. "Are you in danger, miss?"

Evangeline felt a sudden pang. Servants gossiped. What if she told Smith of her danger? Evangeline was sure her maid was the most dedicated of creatures, but if Smith let something drop, news would get back to Lady Bane. Smith would be let go, and Evangeline would lose a valuable ally. "Never mind," she said. "I merely wished to know the extent of your loyalty."

"Oh, miss, you are ever so much nicer than Miss Quinn. I was loyal to her because I had to be. But you. Oh, to you I would be loyal simply because I wish to be."

Evangeline was touched. "Why, Smith, what a kind thing to say!"

"It is true," said the maid. She lowered her gaze. "I would do anything for you, miss. Really, I would."

Like an incoming tide, Evangeline felt the tears in her eyes. "Let us hope it does not come to that," she said softly.

* * *

Nothing more was said about marriage, either by Gerard or his intimidating mama. Life at Deerfield Hall became static and Evangeline allowed herself to relax a little. Gerard took her riding and played billiards with her, the Hales paid a social call. Really, she thought, if it weren't for the fact that she knew her wicked relations regarded her as a prisoner rather than a guest, she would be enjoying herself quite well.

She wrote a letter to her papa, informing him that she was having a pleasant visit with her cousins. "But I am sure they tire of my company, and you, dear Papa, must miss it sorely. Do come and fetch me home soon. Please." The *please* she underlined several times, before signing her name.

As she folded the vellum she hoped her letter would reach its destination. The ball was coming up in a few days. If only Mr. Hale would declare himself, she could be free of her wicked cousins. She could live happily ever after with the Hales. Papa would come to visit often, and he and Mr. Hale would enjoy each other's company greatly, she was sure. Why, if Papa came to fetch her the day of the ball, Mr. Hale would have an opportunity to speak for her and they could announce their betrothal that very night!

And surely Mr. Hale would offer for her. Wouldn't he? Granted, his attentions to her weren't marked, but she couldn't help remember the way he'd held her hand after bowing over it when he and his sister had called on them, as if he'd hated to let it go. And she'd hated to let him release it. His hand was so much bigger than hers, so strong and capable. With her hand in Mr. Edwin Hale's, she would have nothing to fear. She closed her eyes and imagined him curling that strong hand into a fist and striking Gerard on his swarthy smirking face. That vision was almost as pleasant as one that followed it, of herself waltzing in Mr. Hale's arms.

The night of the ball was extremely warm, the heat squeezing the fragrance from the many flowers that adorned Idyllwilde's large saloon. The braces of glowing candles made their small contribution to the high temperature, if only by power of suggestion, and ladies plied their fans vigorously in spite of the many open windows.

Evangeline stood with Gerard and Lord and Lady Bane, waiting for the musicians to tune up, watching the many guests through dazzled eyes. Not only had all the locals turned up to celebrate Miss Plympton's arrival in the neighborhood, but the Hales had also drawn upon their vast acquaintance and imported some gentry and nobility from neighboring shires. Idyllwilde was filled with houseguests, Charlotte had happily informed Evangeline, and the nearby inn had taken the overflow. Looking around, Evangeline saw that her friend had been true to her word and provided an abundance of gentlemen. Surely even the

Amberquail ladies would be able to dance to their hearts' content this night.

Gerard broke in on her reverie. "They are calling the first dance, Cousin. I believe it is mine."

"It is the Quadrille," said Evangeline nervously.

"Yes," agreed Gerard.

Miss Maxim had taught the steps of the four contredanses which made up the Quadrille to her charge, but now that she was at her first ball, about to dance them in public, Evangeline felt panic pushing against the walls of her chest.

As if sensing her nervousness, her cousin smiled at her. "Don't worry, Little Cousin. One must dance one's first dance some time. I shall help you."

And so he did. Not that she needed much help, Evangeline thought proudly when at last Gerard led her off the floor. But her steps had faltered once or twice. She smiled up at her cousin, momentarily forgetting what a villain he was, only thankful that he had gotten her through a nerve-racking experience. "Thank you for helping me," she said shyly.

He bowed. "Not at all. It was my pleasure to serve you."

His mother joined them in time to hear Gerard's words. "Very prettily said, my son." She turned to Evangeline. "You are the envy of every female in the room, my dear. I cannot tell you how many ladies have set their caps for Gerard, but he has been waiting for that one special woman to come along, someone not only deserving, but worthy of our name." She took Evangeline's hand in hers and patted it.

Rather than feeling comforted by such a motherly action, Evangeline felt like a rabbit caught in a trap.

She was spared from replying by the arrival of the squire's son to claim her for the next dance. As she went through the lively motions of the reel, her mind followed her body, spinning dizzily with the implications of Lady Bane's speech. Surely a proposal of marriage would be forthcoming before the next week was out.

She hoped desperately that her father would arrive to take her home before such an uncomfortable scene took place, for kind as her cousin had been during their dance, she knew she could never marry him. Underneath that show of kindness was a man as cold and calculating as Miss Quinn. And worse even than marriage to Gerard was the prospect of Lady Bane, with her sinister, palsied smile and high-handed ways, as a mother-in-law.

The dance ended, and red-faced and huffing, the squire's son led Evangeline off the floor. He returned her to Lady Bane and offered to fetch her punch.

When he returned he seemed inclined to linger, but Her Ladyship shooed him off, reminding him that the next dance would begin shortly and suggesting he find his partner. "That boy is an impertinent young puppy," pronounced Her Ladyship. "He will turn to fat like his papa before he is forty. Not at all a good catch. Ah, well. Perhaps one of the Amberquail ladies might snare him yet."

Lady Bane continued in this vein until another dancing partner presented himself. And then Evangeline was only spared for the duration of the dance, for once she returned to her cousin's side, she was again subjected to a catalog of that partner's flaws. So it continued throughout the evening, and when at last Mr. Hale came to claim a dance, it was all Evangeline could do not to fly from her chair and into his arms.

"I feel as if I have been rescued from a fire-breathing dragon," she confessed as Edwin led her onto the dance floor.

"Her Ladyship has a bit of a reputation for being a dragon," he admitted in an undertone, and she giggled.

The band struck up a waltz, and Edwin took her hand in his and placed his palm on her waist. The contact caused the most amazing prickles to ripple out across her body, and she looked up at him wide-eyed.

His eyes told her he was as affected by the contact as she. "You are the most beautiful woman here tonight," he said. "I am fortunate to have even one dance with you."

"I wish it could be more," she confessed.

"Do you?" he asked eagerly, and she nodded. This widened his smile. "Just so I could keep you from Lady Bane?" he teased. "What is she saying to make you so uncomfortable?"

"She is telling me why every man I dance with would be unsuitable for me," said Evangeline. "Except Gerard, of course. He would be perfect."

The smile faded from Edwin's face. "I suppose you are promised to him. That is, you have an understanding?"

"I certainly have no such thing!" replied Evangeline. "I don't wish in the least to marry Gerard." She looked shyly at Edwin. "Did your sister mention our conversation yesterday?"

"Er, yes," admitted Edwin, looking uncomfortable.

"They are going to force me to marry Gerard. I know it."

"This is hardly the middle ages," said Edwin. "They cannot force you. . . ."

"Oh, but they can. And I don't want to marry Gerard. He frightens me. At the fish pond he tried to—" She broke off and bit her lip, her face glowing cherry red.

Edwin's eyes flew open, then narrowed to angry slits. "A spider, eh?" he growled. "Miss Plympton. Did Bane make ungentlemanly advances to you?"

Evangeline looked away.

"Miss Plympton," said Edwin earnestly. "I wish to know that my sister and I will stand your friends. If you are ever in need of assistance, you need only send a message to me and I shall come to your aid immediately."

The music ended, bringing the conversation to an end as well. And, as far as Evangeline was concerned, it had come to a most satisfactory end. She looked up at Edwin with shining eyes. "Oh, Mr. Hale," she said. "You are the most heroic man I have ever met."

Now it was Edwin's turn to blush. "Nothing of the kind," he said. "Any other man worth his salt would do the same, I assure you."

But Evangeline knew better. Mr. Hale was the stuff of which legends were made. He rescued terrified ladies from bulls, dived into streams to save drowning women. She had no doubt that if she needed him to, he would scale the walls of Deerfield Hall to save her. And not simply because he was noble, but because he loved her. She was certain of it. Surely no man could look at a woman the way Mr. Hale looked at her tonight and not be in love with her!

The rest of the evening passed, framed in a pink haze. As Evangeline took the plate of delictables Gerard had gathered from the supper table, she caught Edwin Hale's admiring eye on her and smiled down at her plate. It was a lovely ball.

On the way home she let the conversation pass by her, cuddling in her corner of the carriage with her memories of the noble Mr. Hale.

* * *

When Gerard suggested they go riding the following morning, Evangeline consented but took along her thoughts of Mr. Hale to keep her company.

"You are quiet this morning, Cousin," observed Gerard. "Are you lost in pleasant memories of the ball?"

Evangeline recalled herself to the present with an effort. "I suppose I was," she said.

"That is the first of many, I daresay," he predicted. "When do you make your social debut in London?"

"Papa is taking me to London for the Little Season in September."

"Where, I am sure, you will take the ton by storm. Of course, they won't let you waltz so freely at Almacks as you did last night."

Evangeline looked questioningly at her cousin.

"The patronesses, you know, must give you permission to do so. Ah, but out here in Devon, what does it matter? Especially," Gerard added with a sly look, "when one is partnered by Mr. Edwin Hale. Tell me, Cousin. Do you wish to be married?"

Here it was, the dreaded offer of marriage! And dropped on her so suddenly! Evangeline felt the blood draining from her face. "Perhaps," she said warily, and added, "someday."

"Parson's mousetrap," muttered Gerard.

Evangeline blinked, sure she had misheard. "I beg your pardon?" she said.

"Never mind, Little Cousin. It was nothing. Would you care to race home?"

Yes, thought Evangeline as they turned their horses, I want to return to my own safe house and my dear papa.

Smith looked at her agitated mistress and rushed to help her out of her riding habit. "Is something wrong, miss?"

"No, no," said Evangeline in tragic accents. "I just wish I were home." And with that she burst into tears.

"Oh, dear," fretted Smith. "Don't cry, miss. You will make your eyes all puffy, you will. Would you like me to ask Cook to make you a tissane?"

Evangeline nodded. She let her maid assist her into a fresh gown, then sat to wait for her tissane and brood over her perilous situation. She had to do something. Perhaps she should bring things to a head, inform her wicked cousin she had no intention of marrying him. Ever. This idea was still stewing in her brain when her abigail arrived with the calming brew.

After drinking it and resting for half an hour, Evangeline felt restored enough to walk in the garden. And in doing so, she encountered Miss Farnham and her charge. Miss Farnham, Evangeline noticed, looked nearly as dejected as she, herself, felt, and Minerva was glaring at her. "Good day, Miss Farnham," she said politely. "Minerva."

"It is always a good day for you," retorted Minerva. "You are an heiress."

"Minerva!" gasped Miss Farnham. "You must apologize to Miss Plympton immediately."

"I am sorry," muttered Minerva.

Evangeline shrugged, trying to pretend she wasn't hurt. As if it were her fault she was an heiress! Really, the child was as wicked as the rest of her family. "Your governess is very kind," she observed casually. "My governess was much stricter. She used to say, 'Rude little girls should be locked in their rooms where they can do no one harm.'"

Minerva said nothing, but Evangeline could imagine she was thinking any number of horrid retorts.

"Minerva, perhaps you would care to watch the fishes," suggested Miss Farnham.

"I already watched the fishes with you and Gerard," pointed out Minerva.

"I would appreciate an opportunity to visit with Miss Plympton," said Miss Farnham gently.

"Very well," Minerva sighed. "I shall go into the maze." She ran off, the two ladies strolling after her at a sedate pace.

Miss Farnham seemed to feel the need to excuse her pupil's behavior. "Minerva is often outspoken in her opinions, but I can assure you, Miss Plympton, she is rarely so rude."

"I am afraid Minerva and I got off on a wrong

foot," said Evangeline. Another strong reason not to marry into this family, she thought.

"She is really a sweet child," insisted Miss Farnham. "When one gets to know her," she added, seeing Evangeline's skeptical look. "She was my first charge." Miss Farnham's expression turned wistful. "This family has been so kind to me. And Mr. Bane—" She broke off, her cheeks a delicate pink.

They had reached the maze now. Evangeline plucked a laurel leaf and said, "Of course, my cousin is very handsome, but I find his character is not so fine as his appearance."

"Oh, but he is a very kind man," protested Miss Farnham. "So thoughtful and considerate, so patient."

Evangeline looked at her companion in surprise. Why, she was in love with Gerard! Oh, wicked, evil man! Had he been trifling with Miss Farnham's affections? She should warn the poor woman, tell her what a villain Gerard was. "Miss Farnham, about Mr. Bane—" she began.

Miss Farnham nodded, her face now a deep crimson. "I know," she said. "I know where his duties lay. I am afraid I have said more than I should. I beg you to forgive me and rest assured that I would never do anything improper."

Evangeline was relieved to hear this. "That is very smart," she approved. "I should hate to see you in a position where you would be hurt."

A snort could be heard from the other side of the

hedge and the two ladies exchanged looks and turned to discussing the weather.

Even as Evangeline sat talking with Miss Farnham, the Hales were discussing her. It had reached the time of day when Charlotte could expect callers coming to express their thanks for the family's hospitality, to relive every delectable dance and review every lady's gown. Their houseguests had all breakfasted, and the clatter of people coming and going from the dining room had at last died down.

"We have yet to find out from Evangeline, herself, the truth of her visit at the Hall," said Charlotte, "but what little she said to you should certainly be enough to convince you that something havey-cavey is going on."

Edwin nodded. "She definitely does not wish to marry her cousin," he said.

Charlotte smiled as her brother tried to hide the triumphant look on his face, then turned serious. "Yes, but rest assured that horrid Lady Bane will do all in her power to force her to do so." Charlotte tapped her chin thoughtfully with her finger. "The ball was a mistake," she announced.

"What?" cried her brother.

She nodded. "Yes, it most certainly was. Well, not completely," she ammended, "for we had a most wonderful time. Especially the Amberquails. I do believe they both danced nearly every dance."

"Yes," said her brother. "And I am sure every male of our acquaintance appreciates the fact that you were sparing with your invitations to our female friends."

His sister ignored this. "What we should have done," she continued, "was to have a dinner. Then we should have been able to observe the family so much better, and I am sure I would have had an opportunity to talk with Evangeline and hear the rest of her story."

"And you think as hostess of a dinner party you will have the opportunity to hear such confidences?" scoffed her brother.

"Well, you may rest assured I shall get little opportunity any other way to talk with her alone. Her cousins keep her on too short a lead."

Edwin nodded. "Just so," he said. "And I see little hope of confidential exchanges at a dinner party. Besides, might I remind you? We just held a ball."

Charlotte looked at her brother as if he were slow-witted. "Edwin. A ball and a dinner party are nothing alike. And besides, we shan't have it until next week."

"Perhaps the Banes will have no desire of our company again so soon," suggested Edwin.

"Then we shall invite Miss Quinn and her mama and papa. As Miss Quinn is about to become a marchioness, I am sure Lady Bane will wish to cultivate her friendship."

Her brother acknowledged this clever strategy with a nod of the head. "An excellent idea," he approved.

"Yes, it is," agreed his sister. She smiled mysteriously. "And if you think that an excellent idea, wait until you see how I manage it so Evangeline can tell us the truth about her visit to her cousins—right under their very noses!"

Chapter
8

Charlotte couldn't be coaxed into telling her brother how she intended to discover what was going on at Deerfield Hall, and her mischievous smile made him nervous. This entire situation made him nervous, he thought as he watched her dance out of the room to see to their guests' amusement. He should settle things man to man with Bane—call him out for his ungentlemanly advances on Miss Plympton and be done with it. Any scheme of Charlotte's was bound to be half cocked. They would all wind up looking like fools, he was sure, and no man liked to look the fool in front of the woman he loved.

His face softened at the thought of Miss Plympton. She was so sweet, so lovely. No wonder Bane had made advances.

Edwin frowned. Something was not right here. Bane was a smart fellow. And no man with anything in his brain box would do something to ruin his chances of marrying an heiress when his family was in need of money, especially a lovely one like Miss Plympton. Perhaps Bane had not made advances. Perhaps Miss Plympton had merely been skittish and misinterpreted some simple gesture.

Edwin shook his head. That was a ridiculous theory. A woman certainly knew when a man was misbehaving! Edwin rubbed his chin thoughtfully. Perhaps Bane had, somehow, said something Miss Plympton took as a threat, something that made her believe she would have to marry him.

Edwin set his jaw. Well, that would never happen. He certainly wouldn't stand back and see her married to someone against her will—especially when he wanted to marry her himself!

His conversation with Gerard at the stables came flying back to haunt him. No, no, no! Miss Plympton simply couldn't be mad. Bane must be mistaken. Or perhaps this claim of madness was a ruse. What better way to frighten off another suitor?

When Miss Plympton and Lady Bane arrived to pay their thank-you call that afternoon, Edwin covertly studied the young lady. Once, she caught him looking at her and smiled. Then she blushed prettily and lowered her eyes. *That* was certainly not the behavior of a madwoman. In fact, it looked very much like the behavior of a young miss encouraging a suitor.

But even if she didn't return his regard, he knew he would risk his reputation, even his life to save this sweet, delicate creature if she were in danger. The word "dinner" caught his ear and he forced his mind back to the subject at hand.

"Just a small gathering of friends," Charlotte was saying. "A ball is very nice, of course, but one really doesn't have the opportunity to converse as one does at a dinner. Wouldn't you agree, Your Ladyship?" Her Ladyship agreed unenthusiastically, and Charlotte continued, "It will be only ourselves and Miss Quinn, our future marchioness, and her parents."

A note of interest appeared in Lady Bane's voice. "Miss Quinn, you say?"

Charlotte nodded. "Yes. Just a small, select gathering. Simply ourselves and the Quinns. If Your Ladyship would deign to honor us with your presence, that is."

"I think we might be able to do so," said Lady Bane, smiling her sinister smile. "What do you say, Evangeline? Should you care to come to the Hales for dinner next week?"

"Oh, yes," breathed Evangeline.

At that moment one of the houseguests wandered in from the gardens and was introduced. As this particular houseguest was no one of consequence, Lady Bane decided it was time to end the visit.

"So good of you to call," Charlotte said politely. To Evangeline, she said, "As is always the case, dear friend, our time together was too short. I am sure we will have much to share when you come to dinner next week, and I shall make sure we have the opportunity to do so." Here she looked at Evangeline meaningfully.

Evangeline caught the message in her friend's gaze and nodded her understanding. As the Banes' landau made its stately progress back to Deerfield Hall, she took hope. Charlotte would find some way for the two of them to finish the conversation Gerard had interrupted. Charlotte knew something was wrong, and she would manage to help her friend. She would send her handsome brother to the rescue. Evangeline knew that if she could just prevent Gerard from proposing before the dinner party, she would be safe.

She envisioned Mr. Hale swooping her up in front of him onto a big white horse, then carrying her into his house, where he took her immediately into his drawing room, dropped on one knee, and proposed marriage. Something intruded on Mr. Hale's proposal, and she realized it was the sound of Lady Bane's voice.

"And it can do you no harm to befriend Miss Quinn," Her Ladyship was saying. "I am sure she is a much more suitable friend than Miss Hale, who is entirely too forward for my tastes. As a marchioness, there is much Miss Quinn could do to advance your social position, and of course, that of your family."

Evangeline considered Miss Quinn to be cold and calculating, and much too high in the instep, but she wisely kept her opinion to herself.

Back at the Hall, she spent the days until she would see her friends again avoiding being alone with Gerard, and, when talking with his mama, trying to stay clear of any subject that might lead to talk of matrimony. This didn't prevent Lady Bane from bringing up the subject. But when she did, Evangeline tried to turn the conversation into other channels as quickly as possible.

Evangeline's behavior didn't go unnoticed, and the disapproving frowns she received for her troubles were disconcerting. As the family made their way to Idyllwilde for the dinner party, she knew she was in Her Ladyship's black books.

Once at the dinner party, however, Lady Bane hid her disapproval well. She was exceedingly cordial to Mrs. Quinn and her daughter. As Mr. Quinn was an ardent sportsman, Lord Bane seemed happy enough talking with him of fishing and guns.

Charlotte moved among her guests like an accomplished hostess, speaking to everyone, making sure no one stood alone. In the midst of her duties she did manage to catch Evangeline's hand and whisper, "I have found a way for you to tell me whether or not you are in danger. Be ready."

She squeezed Evangeline's hand and moved on, leaving her friend to go in to dinner with a roiling stomach.

Dinner seemed interminable, the courses never ending. At last the ladies made their way to the drawing room. As they took their seats, Lady Bane sat possessively next to Evangeline on the sofa, coaxing Miss Quinn to sit on her other side, and Evangeline wondered how on earth Charlotte would manage any communication between the two of them when she was so heavily guarded.

"Well, Miss Quinn," said Lady Bane, "I hope your wedding plans are coming along well."

"They are, thank you," said Miss Quinn politely.

"And where shall you go for your wedding trip?"

"To Italy, I believe."

"Ah, yes. Italy is a beautiful country. And Venice, Venice is beyond description. You will adore it."

"I have heard it is very lovely," agreed Miss Quinn calmly, unimpressed with either Her Ladyship's raptures or her prophetic ability. Evangeline thought again how very cold Miss Quinn was. Just like Gerard.

The gentlemen did not linger over their port, and as soon as they had settled themselves in the drawing room, Mr. Hale turned to his daughter. "Well, my poppet, and what entertainment have you planned for us this evening?"

"I think," said Charlotte with a smile, "that we

shall tax our guests' creative powers a little with a game of charades."

"Splendid idea!" boomed Lord Bane. "Anything is better than sitting about listening to a gaggle of females squealing their way through a song."

"Lord Bane!" chided his wife. "What a perfectly odious thing to say, especially when we have three young ladies present who possess perfectly wonderful voices."

"Well, yes," ammended His Lordship, mildly repentent. "I did not mean to say any of you cannot sing. What I meant was, it is a dashed good idea to do something different for a change."

"I think I should rather sing than make a spectacle of myself," said Miss Quinn.

"Pray, don't worry," said the irrepressible Charlotte. "You need not act out anything if you are fearful."

"I did not say I was fearful," corrected Miss Quinn, insulted.

"I, for one, think it a fine idea," put in Mr. Hale.

"Then, Papa, perhaps you might care to start," suggested Charlotte. "Give us a maxim or a line from some well-known literary work." Here she looked at Evangeline. "Send us a silent message."

Evangeline's eyes widened as the meaning behind her friend's statement hit her. Immediately she put her mind to work.

Mr. Hale stepped to the center of the room and began his charade. The others called out their guesses while he pretended to drop something.

But Evangeline sat silent, searching frantically for a way to tell her friends of the dangerous situation at Deerfield Hall.

"Dropped!" cried Lady Bane.

"Spilt," ventured Miss Quinn, for a moment forgetting her superior position and entering into the spirit of the game.

Mr. Hale pointed to Miss Quinn and nodded vigorously, then pulled down the corners of his mouth and began to rub his eyes with his knuckles. "Crying!" called Charlotte.

"No sense crying over spilt milk," murmured Gerard.

"That is it!" said Mr. Hale, pointing at him. "Clever lad! I thought I would be forced to act out many more words, and I must confess, I had no idea how I should go about showing sense. Well, now, it is your turn."

"I am afraid I shall have to decline," said Gerard. "I am totally lacking in thespian abilities." He turned to Evangeline. "Perhaps my cousin would care to act in my place? Ladies are so good at this sort of thing."

Here was her opportunity! Evangeline nodded her acquiescence, and with a stormy sea in her tummy, she took Mr. Hale's place before the company. She began by folding her hands before her in supplication and looking at the audience (one man in particular) with a pleading expression.

"Help," guessed Edwin.

Evangeline nodded, her face serious, then pointed a finger at her chest.

"Me!" guessed Charlotte. Evangeline nodded and motioned for her to try again. "I," she said.

Evangeline nodded approvingly. Now, how to act out the rest of her message? She stood for a moment, biting her lip, then pretended to gather something and hold it close to her.

"Gather!" cried Mrs. Quinn, and Evangeline shook her head and went through the motion again.

"Hold?" ventured Mrs. Quinn. Evangeline beckoned her to keep guessing in the same vein.

"Clasp," tried Mrs. Quinn.

Evangeline shook her head.

" 'Hold' is closer to the word you want?" asked Charlotte.

Evangeline bobbed her head.

"A different tense perhaps," continued Charlotte thoughtfully.

Evangeline nodded excitedly.

"Held," said Charlotte in somber tones.

Evangeline nodded, thrilled, then continued. Holding her hands before her, she walked with staggering gait and miserable expression, as if being led against her will.

"Captive!" cried Charlotte. "Help! I am being held captive!"

Evangeline nodded. "That is it," she said, looking levelly at Charlotte. As the others applauded the cleverness of both actress and the one who guessed, the two young women sent and acknowledged a message of their own.

"From what famous literary work is that taken?" protested Gerard.

"It is from *The Captive Bride*," said Evangeline. Here, she cast a quick glance at Edwin and caught the look of surprised understanding on his face. She watched him exchange glances with his sister, saw Charlotte give Edwin the slightest of nods, and felt hope soar deep inside her. Now the Hales knew all. They would help her.

"Well, Charlotte," said Mr. Hale, "you have won the right to give us a charade."

Charlotte, still looking at her brother, said, "I shall give it to Edwin. I am sure he must have something he wishes to act upon."

Edwin at first resisted, bashful and reluctant. But at last the ladies persuaded him, and he took the center of the room and went through a variety of motions, pounding his heart, looking soulfully up at something. At last Miss Quinn guessed, "Love?" and Edwin nodded.

"The ladies always know about that, eh?" joked Lord Bane.

Edwin pointed a finger at his chest.

"Me!" guessed his sister. "I . . . my." Edwin was nodding. "My?" she asked, and he nodded again.

Now he motioned with his hand, as if at something high, then got down on one knee. "It is my love," said Gerard softly, "my only love."

Edwin smiled and looked at Evangeline. "Yes," he said, his voice equally soft.

For a moment Evangeline returned his gaze, her eyes glowing, then realized how forward she must appear and dropped her gaze.

"Ah, Shakespeare," sighed Mr. Hale, applauding. "You are really a most clever young man," he informed Gerard.

"Not in the least," replied Gerard. "I only know the signs of a man in love."

Evangeline looked about the room. Miss Quinn's face turned wistful. Edwin was still regarding Evangeline with undisguised admiration. She ventured a pink-cheeked smile at him and shifted her gaze to see Lady Bane smiling at her son approvingly. Had her cousin made that comment for her benefit? Was he trying to make her think he loved her?

The happy warmth fled from Evangeline's heart, leaving her cold with fear. Instinct told her that her days were numbered.

"It must have been a lovely dinner party," prompted Smith later that night.

Evangeline stepped out of her gown, and Smith whisked it away. "Yes, it was," she said, remembering the look in Mr. Hale's eyes after he had done his charade. This was followed by the memory of Gerard's observation about men in love and Lady Bane's evil smirk. Evangeline shivered.

"Oh, dear, you are cold," said Smith, hurrying to ready her mistress for bed.

Only frightened, thought Evangeline.

And the next morning she discovered she had good reason to be. Excitement seemed to radiate off Smith when she answered Evangeline's summons.

"I think I should like to wear my dove-gray gown," said Evangeline.

Smith's face fell.

"Is something wrong with the gray gown?" asked Evangeline.

"Oh, no, miss," said Smith. "It is only that I thought, perhaps, you might wish to wear your pink one. You look so nice in it. The gray seems a little somber, and today I am sure you will want to look your best."

"Today?" said Evangeline sharply. "Why today?"

Smith's cheeks burst into mottled red flames. "Oh, miss, I thought you knew," she said. "I didn't mean to be uppity, really I didn't."

"Know what?" cried Evangeline. "Smith, you must tell me at once!"

"Why, it is nothing terrible. Really, miss. It is only that Mr. Bane intends to propose to you today."

"Nothing terrible!" echoed Evangeline hysterically. "It is nothing short of horrifying!"

"Horrifying!" Smith looked confused and nearly as upset as her mistress.

"How do you know this?" demanded Evangeline.

"I heard it from George, the footman. He overheard Lady Bane and her son talking."

Evangeline collapsed onto her bed. "Oh, dear," she moaned, "what shall I do?" She looked at her maid with pleading eyes, but Smith had no answers. The girl merely stood looking sadly back at her. At last Evangeline heaved a great sigh. "I suppose I shall have breakfast," she said. "I cannot think on an empty stomach."

Lady Bane was already breakfasting when Evangeline came down. This morning her sinister smile looked positively gloating. "How did you sleep last night, my dear?"

"Well enough, thank you," replied Evangeline in dull tones.

Lady Bane examined her guest's face. "You look a trifle peaked," she observed.

"I am homesick," Evangeline said. "I think, perhaps, it is time I return to my papa."

"But you have only just come to us!" protested Her Ladyship.

"I am sure Papa misses me," said Evangeline in a small voice.

"Well, then," said Her Ladyship silkily. "We shall have to write and invite your papa to join us."

This was not what Evangeline wanted, but she decided it would do. After all, the Banes could hardly hold both herself and her father captive once she had refused Gerard. "That would be very nice," she said.

Lady Bane favored her with another smile. "Our two families should be close," she said. "And now, my dear, when you are finished, I believe Gerard wishes to speak with you. He is waiting in the drawing room."

Evangeline gulped. "What does he wish to say?" she ventured.

Lady Bane attempted to look playful. "Such a sly puss! As if you cannot guess. Now, I am sure you are finished. Run along and speak with Gerard."

Evangeline had hardly eaten anything, but the hot bread and eggs on her plate suddenly held no appeal to her. She excused herself and made her way with slow steps to the drawing room. She opened the door to see Gerard pacing before the sofa.

He looked up as she entered and gave her a smile which lacked the power to shine in his eyes. "Good morning, Cousin. I hope you enjoyed your breakfast."

"It was very good," Evangeline managed.

Gerard gave a snort. "But difficult to enjoy with my mother present, preparing you for the slaughter?"

This gave Evangeline a start. "I beg your pardon?"

Gerard waved a careless hand. "Pray, do not mind me, Little Cousin. I am not in the best of moods." He cocked his head and smiled a mocking smile at her, but he seemed to mock himself as he said, "It is nerves, I suppose." He gestured to the sofa. "Would you care to be seated?"

Her heart thrumming wildly, Evangeline perched on the sofa.

Gerard took a seat next to her. Searching her face, he said, "Do you know why you are here, Cousin?"

She stared at him, a bird watching a snake, and nodded.

"Does it frighten you so very much, the prospect of marriage to me?" he asked softly. Evangeline bit her lip, and he smiled, kindly this time. "I am not such an ogre, you know," he continued. "Spoiled, I am afraid, and selfish, but no more so than any other member of the Upper Ten Thousand. But that is not to the point. Evangeline, there is something I must confess."

He moved to take her hand, and she sprang up. "I shan't marry you!" she cried. "And you cannot make me, no matter how long you keep me locked in my room!"

Gerard's mouth dropped. Before he could say anything, Evangeline rushed from the room. Sobbing, she made her way back to her bedroom and threw herself on her bed and shed fat tears of self-pity.

After half an hour of violent crying, she was exhausted. When the gentle tapping came on her door, she could barely manage a weak, "Come in."

Lady Bane entered and Evangeline sat up and looked at her nemesis in horror.

"Oh, dear, look at you," said Her Ladyship. "You have worked yourself into a terrible state. I knew you would be in no frame of mind for a proposal when I saw you at breakfast this morning. A young lady hardly can think logically when she is unwell."

"I am not unwell," protested Evangeline.

"Of course you are," said Lady Bane with a curling lip. "I shall instruct Cook to brew you a tissane, and I am sure you will feel much better by afternoon."

"I shan't ever feel well enough to marry your son," said Evangeline with a defiant lift of her chin.

Lady Bane looked pained. "I am sorry to hear you say that, my dear. We have all been nothing but kind to you since you came, and I cannot imagine why you should have come to take us in such dislike. I shall, of course, write your father this very morning to come fetch you, and send the letter off in the afternoon post."

She left, shutting the door quietly after her, leaving Evangeline feeling foolish and ashamed of her outburst. And confused. Lady Bane had seemed genuinely hurt by what she had said. Could I have misinterpreted her actions? wondered Evangeline. Of course she wished me to marry her son, but what if that was all she'd planned? Perhaps she had never meant to hold me prisoner. Surely, if she planned to keep me here, she would not have offered to send for Papa.

The more Evangeline mulled things over, the more guilty she felt. She wandered to her bedroom window and looked out. In the garden, she could see Gerard and Miss Farnham. There was no sign of the naughty Minerva. Ah, well, Miss Farnham surely deserved a respite once in a while.

Idle curiosity kept Evangeline at the window, watching the couple as they stood by the fish pond. But amazement rooted her where she stood when Gerard took Miss Farnham in his arms and kissed her. "Oh, my!" gasped Evangeline. "No wonder he was reluctant to propose to me."

A knock on her door made Evangeline move from the window, a guilty flush on her face. "Come in," she called.

A maid arrived with a tray bearing a cup and saucer and a steaming pot of herbal drink, poured some for Evangeline, then bobbed a curtsy and left, quietly shutting the door behind her.

Evangeline drank the tea, lay back on her bed, and shut her eyes. Gerard and Miss Farnham, lovers. Who would have thought it? She sighed and let her leaden eyelids fall.

When she awoke, it was with the resolve to apologize to Lady Bane for ever suspecting her of such criminal behavior. Imagine, to think that in real life people ever locked ladies in their room!

She rang for Smith. She would just put on a

fresh gown, have Smith do her hair, then she would go in search of her hostess and apologize profusely, all the while letting Lady Bane know in no uncertain terms, however, that she still had no intention of marrying her son.

A few minutes later her doorknob rattled, and someone tapped on the door. "Miss," called Smith. "Did you ring?"

"Yes, Smith. Come in, please," called Evangeline.

"I cannot," came Smith's muffled reply. "You have locked it."

Evangeline went to the door. The key was missing. She put her hand on the handle and tugged. The door refused to move. Evangeline stared at it. "This cannot be," she said. She tried again. Still, the door refused to open. "It is locked," she gasped. She stared at the door, a wave of terror crashing in on her brain. There was no misinterpreting this. She was, after all, a prisoner!

Chapter 9

"Oh, Gerard," murmured Miss Farnham. "I can hardly believe it. Are you very sure?"

"Mary, dearest, I have never been more sure of anything in all my life," said Gerard. With a smile, he led Miss Farnham to a nearby bench, and they seated themselves, Gerard still holding her hand. "I shall inform my father tonight, after dinner."

"I am afraid your parents, will take the news very hard," fretted Miss Farnham.

"Most likely, they will. But we shall come about. The place has not yet crumbled down around our ears. And I have some new farming techniques I intend to speak with Father about. They may just improve our crop. And that, my dearest, my wonderful future wife, will improve our finances so much more comfortably than my having to marry a madwoman."

Miss Farnham sighed. "I still find it difficult to believe Miss Plympton mad. She always seemed so rational when I spoke with her."

Gerard shrugged. "Perhaps it is only my presence that drives her mad. All the more reason not to marry her." Here he turned again to his beloved. "No, we shall get by. My mother will learn to economize. My father will quit dabbling with the 'change. And we . . ." Here he raised Miss Farnham's hand to his lips. "We shall live happily ever after."

She watched him kiss her hand and smiled. "I sincerely hope so," she said. "And I hope your mama won't hate me too very much."

"Hate you? Impossible! No one could."

"But your mama—" she began.

"Will accustom herself to the news, I assure you. She will have to, for her son has examined his own heart and finds he has not the nobility to lay it on the altar of Deerfield Hall."

"I hope Miss Plympton may not be too disappointed when she realizes what she has lost," said Miss Farnham.

Gerard chuckled. "Miss Plympton, I assure you, will be heartily relieved. For some reason fathomable only to her mad little self, she is terrified of me." He shook his head. "You should have seen how she fled the room when she thought me about to propose. And I only meant to confess to her that

I loved another. Ah, well. Soon enough she will learn how fate has delivered her."

Evangeline, however, was not about to wait for fate to rescue her. By the time Gerard and Miss Farnham had ended their romantic interlude in the garden, the prisoner was slipping a note under the door to her maid. "If ever there was a time I needed your loyalty, it is now, Smith," she hissed under the bottom of the door.

"You know you have it," Smith replied. "I would do anything for you, miss. You have been so very kind to me. But I still don't understand. Why are you locked in your room?"

"It is because I refuse to marry my cousin, Gerard. The Banes wish to have control of my fortune, and they will keep me locked away in this room until I consent to wed him."

"No!" gasped Smith, horrified.

"There is not a moment to lose," continued Evangeline. "You must give this to George or some other servant you trust and tell him to take it to Idyllwilde. The Hales know all and will come to my rescue. I depend on you, Smith."

"I will take it myself," vowed Smith.

"Oh, Smith!" cried Evangeline. "It is such a long way."

"It is only a good stretch of the legs," replied Smith. "And it is the least I can do for you after you have been so good to me."

"Thank you," said Evangeline, and her voice caught on a sob.

"Oh, now, please don't cry," begged Smith. "We will come about. You'll see."

"I hope so," said Evangeline.

Is there anything else you wish me to do, miss?"

"Now that I think on it, yes," said Evangeline. "If they believe I don't know I am locked in it might purchase us some time. Tell Her Ladyship I wish to have dinner in my room."

"But if I go to her with a message from you, she will know I found the door locked," protested Smith.

Evangeline bit her lip and thought hard. "I have it!" she said. "Tell Lady Bane you knocked on my door, and I called for you to go away. Tell her I said my stomach is too upset for food, and I wish only to be left alone. Can you remember all that?"

"Of course, miss," said Smith proudly. "I won't fail you."

"You mustn't," replied Evangeline urgently. "Now, go!"

Charlotte decided enough time had been wasted. Her brother had preached caution, but she knew there was not another moment to lose if Evangeline were to be rescued. Rather than wait for Edwin to return from riding the estate with their father, she readied herself to take the citadel by storm single-handed, putting on her very best afternoon frock, her new straw bonnet, and her lemon kid gloves. She ordered her little pony hitched to the dog cart and made her way to Deerfield Hall, determined to pay a call on the wicked Banes and, if possible, fetch Evangeline home with her. Any excuse would do, and once she had Evangeline safely away, she could stay at Idyllwilde until her papa could come fetch her home.

Grimly did not appear happy to see Miss Hale when he opened the door. Forgetting the fact that Grimley never appeared happy to see anyone, Charlotte took this as yet a further sign of sinister goings-on. She swept past him and asked him to inform Miss Plympton that Miss Hale had come to see her. Grimley showed her into the drawing room, then left to do her bidding.

It was neither Grimley nor Evangeline who entered the drawing room a few minutes later, but Lady Bane. "Miss Hale, how pleasant to see you," she said. "I am so sorry you have taken the trouble to come visit us, all for naught."

"For naught?" repeated Charlotte.

Her Ladyship nodded. "I am afraid so. Our poor little cousin is not feeling well, and is at this moment lying on her bed."

"Is it . . . serious?" asked Charlotte.

"Oh, no, nothing an afternoon of rest cannot cure, I am sure. I shall be happy to give her your regards." Lady Bane stood, ending the interview, and Charlotte had no choice but to take her leave.

On the way home she mulled over the odd circumstances. Evangeline not well? Only the night before she had conveyed the true state of affairs at Deerfield Hall, and today she was

unwell and not receiving visitors. And Lady Bane
was obviously not in the mood for visitors, either.
She had not offered Charlotte so much as a cup of
tea. This was most suspicious. Terrifyingly suspicious! Charlotte gave the reins a slap and urged
her little pony to trot faster.

Smith trembled as she was led into the presence of the wicked Lady Bane. If only, when she'd
looked out the upstairs window, she'd seen Miss
Hale coming up the drive instead of going down it!
She could have given Miss Hale the message from
her mistress and never had to face Lady Bane.
The woman had always frightened her. Now,
knowing the terrible events about to unfold and
how much depended on her, Smith felt her heart
racing round her rib cage and had to swallow hard
before speaking.

"Well, speak up, Smith," demanded Her Ladyship. "I cannot wait all day for you to say our
piece."

Smith gave a wobbly curtsy. "Yes, my lady," she
squeaked. "I have a message from Miss Plympton."

Lady Bane sighed heavily. "Yes, and what is it?"

"Miss Plympton asked me to tell you she is
feeling unwell. I knocked on her door, and she
called for me to go away. She said her stomach is
too upset to think about dinner tonight and asks
only to be left alone." Her speech completed,

Smith bit her lip and waited for Lady Bane's response.

Lady Bane eyes narrowed. "The minx," she muttered. "Very well. She is certainly welcome to remain in her room without dinner. 'Tis no more than she deserves, wicked child." Lady Banes waved Smith away. "Go tell your mistress we shan't disturb her."

Smith fled. Once in the hallway she paused to get her breath. Now for the note. True to her word, she set out for Idyllwilde, trusting no one but herself to deliver her mistress's desperate message.

Charlotte burst through the front door and cast aside her bonnet, calling frantically for Edwin, only to learn from the butler that the men had not yet returned. "They should be," snapped Charlotte. "I'll wager they are snoozing on a grassy bank with their fishing poles propped beside them."

"Yes, miss," said the butler in stately agreement.

She glared at him. "Men!" she snorted and took herself off to the drawing room to pace.

The errants didn't return until late afternoon, calling for tea and cakes as they made their entrance.

Charlotte met them at the drawing room door. "You are finally home," she told them. "I only hope you may not be too late."

Two pair of eyebrows raised. "My dear, what

terrible ill has befallen you since we parted company this morning?" asked the senior Mr. Hale mildly.

"I went to visit Evangeline," said Charlotte.

Edwin's face turned pale. "What has happened?" he demanded.

"Come into the drawing room," said Charlotte. "You shall hear all."

The two men followed her, her brother quiet, her father wondering aloud about what terrible thing could have happened to that nice Miss Plympton when she was in such good hands.

"Oh, but she isn't, Papa!" declared Charlotte. "They want her to marry Gerard so the family can have her fortune. It all looks so honest, but in truth, they are holding her prisoner. And I have learned that things have taken a turn for the worse."

"How do you know?" demanded her brother, his voice sharp.

"Oh, Edwin," moaned Charlotte. "I called today, hoping I would have the opportunity to speak with Evangeline, in fact, thinking I should bring her back here under some pretext, then keep her safe until her papa could come for her."

Edwin rolled his eyes. "I thought we had decided to use some caution," he scolded.

"I decided our friend's situation called for action," replied Charlotte defensively, "so I went. But they would not let me see her."

"Would not let you see her?" echoed Mr. Hale in mild surprise. "Why, wherever did you get such a notion, child?"

"Lady Bane told me Evangeline was unwell and not receiving visitors," said Charlotte.

Edwin visibly relaxed. "Oh, Charlotte, you scared me half to death."

"And so you should be," she snapped. "Don't you see?"

"That Miss Plympton is ill? Yes, that is quite plain."

"Oh, how can you be so clunch-headed!" exclaimed Charlotte in exasperation. "It is plain as a pikestaff something is wrong. How can Evangeline be ill today when she was perfectly fine yesterday?"

"Oh, very easily," said her father, smiling as the butler made his appearance with the tea tray. "That is how it is with illness, you know. One day you are perfectly fine, the next day you are abed with a putrid throat and aching limbs."

Edwin was shaking his head. "No," he said. "I don't believe that is the case here. I think Charlotte is correct."

"Edwin," chided Mr. Hale. "You are far too sensible a young man to let your sister's imagination run away with you."

The discussion was interrupted by the butler, who appeared to announce that Miss Plympton's abigail was at the back entrance bearing a message of some urgency for Miss Hale.

Edwin's face paled.

"Bring the girl here immediately," said his sister.

"Now, we must not jump to conclusions," cautioned Mr. Hale. His children exchanged knowing looks.

A few moments later a red-faced Smith was brought into the drawing room, her hair and clothes damp with sweat. "Have you a message for me?" asked Charlotte, trying to keep her voice level.

The girl nodded. "I carried it myself, miss. Wouldn't trust no one else."

"That was very good," said Edwin. "Now, perhaps you would care to wait in the kitchen and have a glass of cider. I am sure we shall have a message to send back to your mistress." Smith bobbed a curtsy and let the butler lead her away, and Edwin turned to his sister. "Well?"

White-faced, Charlotte handed the missive to him. He read it and gasped, "My God!"

"Did I not tell you as much?" demanded Charlotte, angry. "Here is the proof in her own hand. Locked in her room. Oh, it does not bear thinking of!" She burst into tears, and her father fished out his belcher handkerchief and handed it over to her. "We must do something," she wailed.

Edwin bit his lip, then got up to pace. "Yes, but what? We can hardly go charging over to Deerfield Hall and bring her out by force."

"I am not sure either your brother or myself

would win a confrontation with the baron," said Mr. Hale.

"How else shall we be able to set her free?" protested Charlotte.

Edwin ran his fingers through his hair. "We shall have to find a plan to spirit her away," he said.

Charlotte snapped her fingers. "Her maid! Of course, it is all so simple." Beaming she tugged the bellpull to summon the butler.

Ten minutes later Smith stood once more before the Hales. "So you see, all you have to do is get the key to Miss Plympton's room, unlock the door, and take her down the servants' stairs. We shall have a carriage waiting at the end of the drive."

"But I cannot get the keys," said Smith in a small voice.

Charlotte's face fell. "What? Whyever not?"

"Because the housekeeper wears them on her belt."

"She must have a ring in the pantry where she hangs them sometimes."

Smith shook her head. "I have never seen them out of her sight."

Charlotte frowned and sank back into her chair. "What now?" she moaned.

Edwin, too, looked dejected. "I haven't the foggiest," he confessed. "Short of jumping out the window, it would appear she is trapped."

Charlotte looked at her brother as if he had just said something very brilliant. "That's it!" she declared.

Chapter
10

Charlotte said to Smith, "I shall write a note for you to take to your mistress. Tom can drive you back in the dogcart."

Edwin eyed his sister nervously. "Would you mind telling me what you have in mind?"

She sent Smith on her way and gave him a smile that was decidedly sly. "I have in mind a most dramatic rescue, I assure you—one that will be talked about for years to come."

Jem Mortimer, the gardener at Deerfield Hall, looked nervously over his shoulder. He must have been bloomin' mad to let that young woman, Smith, talk him into this nonsense. It would as good as cost him his job, he'd told the girl when she'd put forth her strange request.

Smith had insisted it was a matter of life and death, and had gone on to assure him that he was to have a job at Idyllwilde if he were turned off, and at twice the wage he was receiving here at the Hall.

But now, as Jem peered into the darkness and saw nothing but the black shapes of bushes, he wondered if the girl had been having a bit of fun at his expense. A fine fool he should look if he were found sulking about outside the house with only this ladder for company. He could almost hear his friends laughing and asking him was he planning an elopement? He frowned and strained his ears. Was that horses' hooves he heard in distance? He hunkered down to wait.

High above him Evangeline peered out her open window, searching for some sign of her rescuer. Charlotte had instructed her to have her valise packed and her window open. When night fell, Edwin would come to save her. Night had fallen. Where was Edwin?

She looked to the ground below. It seemed such a long way down. The thought of descending all that distance on a wobbly ladder made her queasy. What if the ladder fell? What if she lost her footing? No, she told herself, resolutely, Mr. Hale would not let her fall.

Her eyes had become accustomed to the darkness, and she thought she made out the shape of a man squatting on the ground. "Mr. Hale?" she called softly.

The figure jumped and shrank back against the wall of the house.

"Oh, dear," fretted Evangeline and wished Smith were with her. She had not heard from Smith since she'd slipped the note from Charlotte under the bedroom door and received her instructions, and now Evangeline felt miserably isolated. Hugging herself, she sat down on her bed. "Hurry, Mr. Hale," she pleaded.

It seemed an eternity before she heard what she thought was the sound of someone calling. Rushing to the window, she heard it again. "Miss Plympton!" called a male voice, straining to be quiet yet heard. She leaned out the window and saw her hero standing in the flowerbed below with the gardener. And there was Charlotte, too!

"We're here to help you, dear," called up Charlotte in a hoarse whisper.

"Oh, thank heaven," breathed Evangeline.

As Charlotte called words of encouragement, the two men heaved the long ladder against the stone wall. Edwin looked at it and scowled. "It doesn't reach all the way to the window," he said.

"I didn't think it would," said the gardener.

Edwin observed the ivy climbing up the wall and tangling about Evangeline's window. "Would that ivy be strong enough to hold me?" he asked.

The man shrugged. "Don't know, sir. 'Tis right strong stuff, but I've never tried to hang from it, so I couldn't say."

Edwin rubbed his chin. "Well, we'll have a go at it," he decided and put his foot to the ladder.

Evangeline watched him climb. "Do be careful, Mr. Hale," she cautioned.

From below, Charlotte and the gardener watched Edwin's progress. Charlotte held her breath as her brother grabbed a handful of ivy from below Evangeline's room and pulled himself up from the ladder. Both women screamed, as with a rustle, the ivy pulled away from the crumbling wall, sending a shower of stone crumbs to the ground, and leaving Edwin swinging precariously.

"Grab the ladder, sir," called the gardener, trying to steady the contraption from below.

Edwin hooked a foot onto the ladder, and now both ladder and man swayed as Edwin clung to the dangling ivy. Evangeline disappeared into her room, and Charlotte called up, "Oh, Edwin, be careful!"

Edwin seemed to swing and teeter for some time before Evangeline reappeared in the window. "Here," she called and threw out what appeared to be a bedsheet. "Grab on to this. I have tied the end of it to the leg of the wardrobe."

Edwin made a wild grab for the swinging fabric, and his sister buried her face in her hands.

"'Tis alright, miss. 'E's up," said the gardener.

Charlotte raised her face to see Edwin scrambling over the window ledge. "Thank heaven," she breathed.

"Miss Hale," said a voice at her elbow. "How kind of you to call."

With a gasp Charlotte whirled around to find Gerard standing behind her, wearing an amused look. "Is this, perhaps, an elopement?"

The blood drained from Charlotte's face, and for a moment she swayed, as if she might faint. She grabbed the ladder with one hand and swallowed hard, then drew herself up to her full five feet and replied, "No, sir. It is a rescue!"

An amused eyebrow cocked up. "A rescue, is it?" He turned and called. "I have found the source of the scream."

Lord Bane appeared from around the corner of the house. He stared, first at Charlotte, then at the ladder and his quaking gardener. "What the devil?" he exclaimed.

"Gerard! Who is out there?" came Lady Bane's voice. "Is someone hurt?" Now Her Ladyship came picking her way across the grass, a shawl wrapped around her shoulders. She stopped at the sight of Charlotte and stared as if at some horrible, incomprehensible vision. "Miss Hale," she gasped. She took in the ladder and her eyes narrowed. "What is the meaning of this, young lady?"

"My papa knows we are here," said Charlotte stoutly, "and if we do not return with Evangeline within the hour he shall come with men to fetch us."

"Whatever do you mean?" demanded Lady Bane. She shivered, then scowled. "Come," she said, casting a look at the gardener that made him quake in his boots, "this is hardly the place to talk. We shall go inside."

"Would you care to have me fetch Mr. Hale from Evangeline's bedroom?" asked Gerard mildly.

Lady Bane gasped. "Good heavens!" She raised her chin and looked down her nose at Charlotte. "Have you no shame?"

Up in Evangeline's bedroom the two lovers faced each other, oblivious to what was happening beneath the window. "You came," whispered Evangeline.

"Of course I came," said Edwin, "Miss Plympton."

He held out his arms, and Evangeline rushed into them, laid her cheek on his chest, and indulged herself in a good cry.

"There, now," soothed Edwin. "You will be safe soon."

Evangeline looked up at him. "Now that you have come, I know I will be safe."

This trusting remark, combined with the worshipful look on that beautiful face was too much for mortal man to resist, so Edwin Hale, being as mortal as the next man, gave in to temptation and kissed Miss Plympton full on her delicate little lips.

"Oh, Mr. Hale," she sighed.

"Yes, my love?" he whispered.

"That was wonderful."

"I agree," he said and kissed her again.

The knock on Evangeline's door and Gerard's voice brought them back to their senses, and they pulled apart from each other with a jerk.

"Please come out, Cousin," commanded Gerard's voice. "Miss Hale and my parents are waiting in the drawing room."

Evangeline and Edwin looked at each other in panic. "The ladder," hissed Evangeline and ran to the window, Edwin behind her. But the ladder was nowhere to be seen. Only the bedsheet remained, dangling over a long, long expanse of wall. The two looked at each other. "We are trapped," said Evangeline in a hopeless voice.

"Do you come out or do I come in?" demanded Gerard. "We shall get you safely out of this house," Edwin assured her. "Come." With a protective arm about her shoulder he led her to the door.

She pulled on the handle. "It is still locked," she said, looking at Edwin in puzzlement.

"Come, Cousin," came Gerard's voice. "I grow tired of these games. Unlock your door."

"But I cannot!" cried Evangeline. "I have not got the key. As you should well know since it was your mother who locked me in!"

There was a long silence on the other side of the door. "That is ridiculous," said Gerard at last.

"It is true, Bane," called Edwin. "There is no key here. We are very much locked in."

"Very well," came the reply in clipped tones. "I

shall return momentarily. I depend on you, Hale, to act the gentleman until I return."

Edwin seemed to puff up with indignation. "You, of all people, sir, should not speak to me of acting the gentleman!" He turned to Evangeline and said, "I don't understand. If they locked you in, why did your cousin think you had the key?"

Evangeline frowned, her mind working for explanations. One came to her and she raised a fearful face to Edwin. "What if they have lost it?" she said in a small voice.

"Then I shall carry you down the ladder," said Edwin firmly.

As Gerard was making his way downstairs, he met Miss Farnham. "Oh, Gerard!" she cried. "Such a terrible trick your sister has played."

"I am sorry, my dear, but I cannot hear about it now. Miss Plympton is locked in her room with Mr. Hale."

"With Mr. Hale!" repeated Miss Farnham in shocked terms.

Gerard took her hand. "I promise you we will have this all settled in no time, then you may tell me all about Minerva."

"But, Gerard—" began Miss Farnham.

"My dear, please," said Gerard in strong tones. "Can you not see we have a very serious situation here?"

"Yes, I can," replied his beloved in equally

strong tones. "And I hold the key to the problem," she added, holding up a key.

Gerard stopped and stared wide-eyed at it. "Is this what I think it is?" he asked.

She nodded. "Minerva somehow managed to steal it from Miss Plympton's door and locked the poor woman in her room. She only just now confessed to me."

Gerard took the key. "Come," he said, turning back the way he'd come. "We'd best set my cousin free immediately. Did Minerva say why she did such a wicked thing, something she knew would get her in great trouble?"

"I am afraid she wished to punish Miss Plympton. You see, she has hated her from the day she came."

"That has been evident," said Gerard, his face grim.

Miss Farnham laid a hand on his arm, stopping him. "It is because of me that she hated Miss Plympton."

"You?"

Miss Farnham nodded. "Minerva is a very observant child. I think she knew I loved you long before I knew it myself. And she had heard us talking on several occasions. She had heard you call Miss Plympton the goose that laid the golden egg. She knew you were to offer marriage to Miss Plympton, and she had hoped that you and I . . ." Here Miss Farnham blushed prettily, and Gerard covered her hand with his. This gave Miss

Farnham strength to continue. "At any rate, Miss Plympton made a comment only yesterday that naughty little girls should be locked in their rooms, and Minerva thought that poor Miss Plympton was being very naughty in trying to take you from me, so she decided to give Miss Plympton the very punishment she suggested."

Here Gerard burst out laughing. "Oh, that is rich! What a farce. Here is Miss Plympton believing my mother locked her in her room."

"Whyever would your mother do such a thing to Miss Plympton?" asked Miss Farnham, confused.

"Why, for refusing to marry me, of course."

"Oh, my," said Miss Farnham.

"Yes," said Gerard.

"Oh, I do hope Miss Plympton won't be too terribly angry about all this," fretted Miss Farnham.

"I am sure she will be willing to forgive and forget," said Gerard.

"Do you think your mama will be very angry with Minerva? It was terribly naughty, I know, but she did it for me."

"I am afraid Minerva will have to be punished," said Gerard. "After all, she cannot go about locking every visitor she takes in dislike in their room." Miss Farnham looked upset by this, and he patted her hand reassuringly. "Don't worry. Minerva is made of very sturdy stuff. She will survive any punishment my mother chooses to dish out, I assure you. Now," he said briskly. "I think you had best hurry to the drawing room. I will join you as soon as I have set the prisoners free. I hope, between the two of us, we will be able to untangle this coil."

"Very well," said Miss Farnham, and set off, leaving Gerard to fetch Evangeline and Edwin.

Edwin was the picture of bristling offense when Gerard opened the bedroom door. "Thank you," he said frigidly. He picked up Evangeline's valise with one hand and put the other under her elbow. "And now, I believe my sister and I will be taking Miss Plympton home with us."

"I think, perhaps, you may wish to take a drink of port in the drawing room and hear how Miss Plympton came to be locked in her room," said Gerard, not looking in the least abashed.

"I think not," said Edwin stiffly.

"Oh, but I must insist," said Gerard with a smile. "It should prove most enlightening, and I must confess I could use enlightening on a few things, myself."

Edwin and Evangeline exchanged looks. Edwin gave Evangeline the slightest of nods, and she said, "Very well," and swept out of the room.

They entered the drawing room to find Miss Farnham talking earnestly to an audience of two and one half. Charlotte sat wide-eyed, gripping the arms of her chair. Lady Bane sat tipped in one corner of the sofa, her eyes closed and her husband next to her, chaffing her hand. The hartshorn sitting on a nearby table silently announced that

Her Ladyship had endured a great shock. Evangeline's eyes saw the sheet of vellum lying on the half-conscious woman's lap and knew what that shock had been. "My letter to Charlotte," she said in a weak voice and sank onto the nearest chair.

"Yes, young woman," snapped Lord Bane. "*Your* letter. Your letter it was which put this poor woman in a swoon."

Edwin sprang to Evangeline's defense. "And it was your family's cruelty which forced her to write such a letter. Locking her in her room!"

"Locked in her room?" roared Lord Bane. "Such poppycock! As if we would do such a thing."

"Oh," moaned Lady Bane, returning to the land of the living.

"I was just now telling them about Minerva's part in this," said Miss Farnham to Gerard.

"Yes, there is the real culprit," said Gerard, turning to Edwin. "I am afraid Minerva did not much care for my cousin. Minerva got hold of the key to Evangeline's room and locked her in."

"Why would Minerva do such a thing?" demanded His Lordship. "And why the devil shouldn't she like Evangeline?"

"Simply because she did not wish me to marry Evangeline. In her eyes our cousin was a usurper, come to take the place of one she thought infinitely more suited to me." The smile he gave Miss Farnham caused both Charlotte's and Evangeline's eyes to widen in amazement. "Wouldn't you say that is so, Mary?"

Miss Farnham blushed and murmured agreement.

Lady Bane's eyes widened and she reached for her husband's hand as if preparing for a great shock.

"Then, did you never mean to marry Evangeline?" Charlotte asked Gerard.

"There has been some talk of marriage between our two families," he said. "But my cousin and I found we would not suit." He smiled at Evangeline. "I am afraid my heart already belonged to another before you came to visit, Cousin. I think, perhaps, that news comes as a relief to you?"

Evangeline blushed and stammered. "Then when you spoke to me . . . you were not trying to propose?"

Gerard shook his head. "Only to put your mind at ease." He turned to look at his mother. "I am afraid I have an entirely different bride in mind, Mother. I am going to wed Miss Farnham."

A moan escaped Lady Bane, and with a flutter of eyelids she fainted again. "Curse it all, Gerard!" muttered his father. "We just got her brought round." He leaned over his wife and grabbed the hartshorn.

"Then I was never really in danger?" asked Evangeline in a small voice.

"In danger?" Gerard looked at her, puzzled.

She looked around the room. Miss Farnham looked confused. Charlotte stared at her, stunned. Edwin was frowning. What a fool she'd been!

What a silly little fool! She had only to look on her friends' faces to see what they thought of her. And to think Mr. Hale had scaled the wall of Deerfield Hall, risked life and limb to rescue her . . . from nothing! She pressed her hand to her mouth to muffle a sob and ran from the room, unable to bear one more minute of public shame.

Two footmen lingered about the hallway, and she sped by them and up to her room where she shut the door and wished she had the key to lock it. Even the servants knew! Soon all of Devon would know about silly Miss Plympton who came to visit her relatives and imagined herself a prisoner.

The loyal Smith came to her and tried to comfort her, helping her into her nightgown, telling her anyone could make an honest mistake, confirming her suspicions that the entire household knew of her foolishness.

"And anyway, this was not an honest mistake," sobbed Evangeline. "It was foolish and cruel. Oh, how could I have been so stupid? How could I ever have suspected such a thing?"

"I don't know, miss," said Smith. "But I will tell you this much. Lady Bane frightens me, and that's the truth."

Evangeline was inconsolable. She knew her relatives would never forgive her.

She could only hope that her papa would come soon to take her away. Once home, she would never again go about in society. Instead, she would devote the rest of her life to her papa. She would convince him to take a little cottage somewhere, where she could live a hermit-like existence and never have to face a member of polite society. For surely by the Little Season news of the mad Miss Plympton would be all over London.

She awoke late the next morning with a dull headache and the firm resolution to find her hostess and beg her forgiveness.

Smith was putting the finishing touches on her hair when a timid knock came on her bedroom door. "Come in," she called, and a very nervous-looking Minerva sidled around the door and into the room.

"Yes, Minerva?" said Evangeline, trying to keep the animosity from her voice.

"Mama told me I had to come apologize," said Minerva.

"It is accepted," said Evangeline shortly.

"I am truly sorry," said Minerva. She ventured farther into the room. "Gerard is to marry Miss Farnham," she announced.

"I am happy for them," said Evangeline. "At least someone will have their happy ending," she said wistfully.

Minerva seemed to take this as encouragement and drew closer to the dressing table. "Mama told Gerard that he will now inherit a crumbling wreck of a house, but Gerard told her that at least he would enjoy living in it with the woman he loves, and he's sure we'll all manage just fine. And

Mama said at least Miss Farnham is a sensible woman who knows how to economize. And Miss Farnham is still to be my governess. For a while, at any rate. And Miss Farnham has promised she will still spend time with me after she and Gerard are married."

The child stood for a moment, watching Smith tie a ribbon in Evangeline's hair. "Miss Farnham has prettier hair than you," she said and ran off.

Evangeline and Smith exchanged looks in the mirror, and Smith giggled.

But Evangeline, remembering the task that lay ahead of her, could only muster the tiniest of smiles. Her toilette finished, she went in search of Lady Bane.

She found Her Ladyship sitting in the drawing room, stitching, Miss Farnham bearing her company.

Lady Bane looked up coldly at her. "Good morning, Evangeline. I trust you slept well?"

No more "my dear," thought Evangeline. She supposed Miss Farnham was now "my dear," and after having a mad houseguest who imagined you to be an arch villainess, a poor gentlewoman must seem a very fine addition to the family, indeed.

Evangeline cleared her throat and launched into her apology. "I have come to beg Your Ladyship's forgiveness," she said. "I don't know how I could have come to so wrongly interpret all your kind actions."

"Perhaps you were too well read," observed Her Ladyship.

Evangeline hung her head.

"Well, I am sure it is all in the past now," said Lady Bane in the stiff tone that told Evangeline that the horror of her misbehavior would be carried far into the future.

Evangeline didn't know quite what to say to this, but she was spared from replying as Grimley chose that moment to make his entrance. "Mr. Hale is here to see Miss Plympton," he announced.

"Oh, no," gasped Evangeline. "I cannot see him."

"Tell Mr. Hale that Miss Plympton is not at home," commanded Lady Bane.

"No, wait," said Miss Farnham, then blushed at her own boldness. "That is, Miss Plympton, I think you should see Mr. Hale."

"Oh, I cannot," said Evangeline. "Not after last night. How could I face him?"

"He clearly has found the courage to face you," said Miss Farnham gently.

Evangeline bit her lip, and Miss Farnham turned to Grimley. "Please conduct Mr. Hale to the library and tell him Miss Plympton will be with him momentarily." Excusing herself to Lady Bane, she left the sofa and came to Evangeline. "Don't make the mistake I nearly made," she said, squeezing Evangeline's arm. "Pride is cold comfort. Reach out and take your happiness like a true heroine."

Evangeline set her jaw in resolution. She would, at least, go and see what Mr. Hale had to say.

The sound of carriage wheels drifted in from the open window. "Now, I wonder who that might be," said Her Ladyship in perturbed tones.

At that moment Grimley appeared to tell them. "Mr. Plympton has arrived, Your Ladyship."

"Papa!" cried Evangeline. She rushed past Grimley to her father, who had appeared in the doorway.

"Here now, my little buttercup. Are you surprised to see your old papa?" cried the little man, hugging her. "How do, Augusta," he said as an afterthought.

"Papa, what a wonderful surprise!" declared Evangeline.

"I thought you might be ready to come home," said her father, telling her by his look that he had received her letter.

"Well, now you are here, come in and sit down," said Her Ladyship in resigned tones. "I suppose we had best bring Mr. Hale into the drawing room, as well."

"Mr. Hale!" Evangeline was gone, leaving her father to gape after her.

Edwin Hale sat in the library, fidgeting with his watch fob. At the sight of Evangeline he jumped up from his chair. "Miss Plympton," he said stupidly.

The way she entered the room reminded him of

a skittish colt. "Mr. Hale," she said in a small voice.

"Are you feeling well this morning?" he asked. Stupid thing to say! That made it sound as if last night had been an illness, an aberration. He bit his lip.

Evangeline nodded. "I suppose I am," she said. She took a seat and lowered her eyes to stare at the floor. "I feel so foolish, so incredibly stupid."

"It was an honest mistake, one anyone could have made," said Edwin earnestly. He had thought to comfort her, but his words seemed to have the opposite effect. Her lower lip began to tremble, making him feel equally distressed. In two steps he was kneeling before her. "Miss Plympton . . . Evangeline. Please don't cry." Now she was crying in earnest. "Don't cry, dearest," he said, moving to gather her in his arms.

"Oh, I wish I had never come here," she sobbed. "My papa has come for me, and I am going to have him buy a cottage far away from everyone, for I never want to see another person as long as I live!"

"Oh, but you cannot leave," protested Edwin, alarmed. "Have your papa come and stay with us. We shall have a house party."

"Oh," wailed Evangeline. "I cannot face your family. I cannot face anyone in the neighborhood. What will they all think of me?"

"Why, only that you have great imagination," said Edwin gently. "And as for wishing you'd never come here. Think how horrible that would have been, for if you had not come here, we might never have met."

Evangeline sniffed, and Edwin gallantly produced a handkerchief for her. "I felt such a fool last night," he confessed. "I thought, what will Miss Plympton think of me, scrabbling up walls and into windows?"

"Why, I thought you were the bravest man I have ever met," said Evangeline earnestly.

"Do you still?" he asked eagerly. "Do you think enough of me to marry me?"

"Marry you! Oh, can you really wish to marry me after I have behaved like such a silly wigeon?"

Edwin pulled away and took her by the shoulders. "There was nothing silly about the way you behaved," he insisted. "You obviously misunderstood many of your cousin's actions, but you always showed great courage. And cleverness! If you had not thrown out the bedsheet to me last night, I am sure I would have fallen and broken my neck."

"Oh, Edwin," gasped Evangeline, then blushed at her use of his Christian name.

He smiled. "I like Edwin," he said. "But I prefer 'dearest.'"

"Oh, Edwin, dearest," she cooed. "How wonderful you are. I am sure I don't deserve such a man."

"Then you will marry me?"

"Only if you promise never to let me read

another novel ever again," said Evangeline, a twinkle in her eye.

Edwin smiled. "I think I can assure you that you will have little time for reading once we're married. You see, Charlotte thinks it would be a good idea if you and she were to write a book together."

Evangeline giggled. "And what should we call it?" she asked.

Edwin cocked his head. "Why, *The Captive Husband,* of course."